THE YEAR OF THE FRENCH EXCHANGE STUDENT

Wes Perrin

Cold Tree Press

Nashville, Tennessee

For other quality books published by Cold Tree Press visit our web site:
www.coldtreepress.com

Sweater Photography David Bailey

Library of Congress Control Number: 2005932340

Published by Cold Tree Press
Nashville, Tennessee
www.coldtreepress.com

9/10/05

Birdie!

From one
wannabe writer
to a ~~genuine~~ Genuine *
Author—all
Best wishes for
your Next Best Seller.

W.G. Pearson

* sorry to
so sloppy

Author's Note

Although anyone who frequented the halls of Parkrose HS in the 50's will recognize in this book a number of similarities to actual happenings, *The Year of the French Exchange Student* is a work of fiction, not a memoir. The characters may remind readers of classmates, but they are not meant to be actual representations of real people. For example, if you try to "guess who Williams is supposed to be," you will be disappointed, because he—like all the others in the book—is simply the product of my imagination. "Well, what about Perry Palmer?" you might ask. "Isn't he an awfully lot like you?" Yes, he is, but even Perry is his own unique personality with traits different from the author.

Without question, however, those who comprised the Parkrose High School Class of 1955, did provide the inspiration for this book. Without them, there would be no story like this one. So, thank you very much, fellow Broncos. I'm in your debt for some wonderful experiences and special, long-lasting memories. It was indeed, "The best of times." This book is gratefully dedicated to all of you.

With special thanks to Jack and Loraine Chapman, Bob and Ann Dueltgen, Jerry Hilton and to my wife, Joanne, PHS Class of '56.

"How blissfully little did seem to matter in the Fifties. Politics, religion, class—all beside the point. Young lives then, once Eisenhower had settled for a draw in Korea and McCarthy had self-destructed like a fairy tale goblin, seemed to be composed of timeless simplicities and old verities..."

—John Updike "The Other"
(Trust Me Short Stories)

"It was the best of times, it was the worst of times, it was the age of wisdom, it was the age of foolishness, it was the epoch of belief, it was the epoch of incredulity, it was the season of light, it was the season of darkness, it was the spring of hope, it was the winter of despair."

—Charles Dickens
"A Tale of Two Cities" (1859)

Prologue

In 1859, Charles Dickens opened *Tale of Two Cities* by writing "It was the best of times, it was the worst of times, it was the age of wisdom, it was the age of foolishness." Little did he know his words would apply equally well nearly 100 years later. Nor could he have guessed that American high school students would be staring at his prose on a regular basis. When the school year began for the class of 1955, at New Rose High School in Oregon's Willamette Valley, *Tale* was the first book assigned in senior English class. To say the least, it was not a popular choice. The seniors regarded it as ancient—pages and pages of stuff that had nothing to do with their daily routine.

Most of these teen-agers were aware, albeit dimly, that their era while maybe not completely the best of times, was still pretty okay. Ordinary and boring, but still not bad. Among families, "There was a conviction, unstated but always there, that life was good and was going to get better," wrote David Halberstam in his book, *The Fifties*. Collectively kids felt the world was waiting for them, and once they graduated, significant and possibly exciting changes would occur in their lives.

After all it was a time when jobs were plentiful (unemployment was 4.4% nationally), and welfare cases rare. There weren't any deep religious or ethnic differences to worry about. The town's only "minorities" were the Italian truck farmers along the river and the few dozen black families who had arrived during the war to work in the shipyards and lived clustered around the river front at the north end of town. The streets were clean, and lawns, although rarely weed-free, were carefully and regularly mowed. No one seemed outlandishly wealthy or abysmally poor. A casual visitor would likely assume New Rose might be "an awfully good place to raise kids." To an outsider, if it weren't the best of times, it sure seemed a reasonable facsimile.

Of course, at the high school level, there were some loose bricks in this wall of contentment. There was the occasional teenage pregnancy, the hushed-up beer party, the random fistfight behind the football bleachers, the drag race ending in a bone-shattering crash. Everyone "got along fine," or so it seemed, but "social service" clubs flourished—thinly disguised fraternities/sororities that fueled smugness and prejudice among the more popular.

More importantly, flickering on black & white television sets were fuzzy media images of civil injustice in the South and ominous warnings about nuclear fallout. Yet, somehow those problems seemed far away and unreal, more like a Hollywood movie. Certainly they didn't touch New Rose lives. It would take until December 1, 1955, before Rosa Parks would refuse to leave her seat on the Montgomery, Alabama bus line. And it would be several years more in New Rose before public embarrassment and lack of patronage would force the closure of the racially tainted Coon Chicken Inn.

Many would argue that the period did qualify as an age of wisdom—at least as far as new inventions were concerned. Bursting forth from scientific labs were Salk's polio vaccine, transistors, Sputnik, tranquilizers, automatic transmissions, vitamin-fortified cereals, roll-on deodorant the first non-smear lipstick, and of course, *the pill*.

And it clearly qualified as an age of foolishness. It was a time when Ed Sullivan reigned as the "unofficial minister of culture" in America with his *Toast of the Town* TV show. A time when the hit songs included *The Ballad of Davey Crockett, Tweedle Dee, Cherry Pink* and *Apple Blossom White,* and *Tuitti Frutti.* A time that saw the introduction of Kentucky Fried Chicken, Ann Landers, and Disneyland. A time of poodle skirts, panty raids and ducktail haircuts.

To the seniors struggling that year to stay awake in Miss Greystone's class, none of Dicken's words really hit home. They thought Dickens was an old geezer who couldn't possibly understand their fabulous 50's. They agreed, sort of, that they were in the season of light and the spring of hope, but as for the season of darkness and the winter of despair, well, somebody else would have to worry about those. After all Ike was in charge, and we were the greatest country in the world. Yes, there was that Korea business, but the truce had been signed, and as far as Indo China was concerned, the French could worry about it. The seniors were blissfully unaware that life was about to speed up dramatically for them, and not in the ways they daydreamed.

Change, especially significant or radical change, was not a notion embraced by their parents or teachers. Mr. Beasely, the New Rose principal, liked to tell the PTA ladies, "The only person who welcomes change is a wet baby." The ladies, most of them, would laugh politely, but it was a nervous chuckle because they recognized that, in spite of their best efforts to the contrary, things in New Rose were changing. Most folks had television sets now, and it was obvious, "plain as the nose on your face," to quote Principal Beasely, that the whole world was moving in new directions.

But all that could wait, because for one school year—the year of the French Exchange Student—New Rose High School remained frozen in time. And that's what this tale is all about.

—*Wes Perrin*
June, 2005

THE YEAR
OF THE
FRENCH
EXCHANGE
STUDENT

Wes Perrin

★ NEW ROSE BUD ★

The Student Newspaper of New Rose High School

Volume X, Number 9   *Friday, May 6, 1954*

(Last Edition of the School Year)

French Exchange Student Coming to Join Sr. Class

Principal Barclay Beasely at last week's Assembly said he had received word that a foreign exchange student from France would be coming to New Rose next fall. "Her name is Francoise," he announced, "and based on her picture I would say she is very 'trey bone.' I want all you students to welcome her warmly when she arrives. No snide comments about 'frogs' will be tolerated."

"This is really exciting because the theme of this year's prom is "Evening in Paris," said Penny Dusenberg who is charge of decorations. "We're going to make everything really French and Parisian-like. We've even asked the chaperones to wear berets."

Student Body Officers Elected for Next Year

In an election that was decided by only six votes, Raymond Kingfisher was picked as SB President for the coming school year. Orville Duprey Jr. came in second. "I promise to do a bang-up job for New Rose High," said the smiling winner.

There was one surprise. Write-in candidate Perry Palmer was elected sergeant-at-arms. "Beats me," said Perry when asked why he had won.

"Maybe because my friends, Ron Johnson and Platy Sherwood pushed this write-in thing." Another friend, Danny Williams, claimed it was "manifest destiny."

August, 1954 News Flashes

Roger Bannister of England defeats Australia's John Landy in Vancouver, B.C. to win the "Mile of a Century Race." Time: 3:58.8.

Assistant Labor secretary James Wilkins becomes the first Negro to attend a weekly cabinet meeting in Washington D.C., filling in for absent Labor Secretary James Mitchell.

Studebaker Corporation workers voted at a mass meeting in South Bend, Indiana, to accept a wage cut of $12-20/week to help the firm recover from a sales slump.

The first issue of Sports Illustrated is published.

A B-52 "Stratofortress" air bomber is flown for the first time.

Chapter One
Nocturnal Maneuvers

Pausing to catch his breath, Perry Palmer, age 17, could feel the moisture oozing through the canvas sides of his Chuck Taylor sneakers. He scowled and squinted into the moon-less summer night. His bifocaled eyesight, not all that terrific in daylight, was even worse after dark. He could clearly hear the swish-swish of dozens of oscillating lawn sprinklers and the nonstop chirping from legions of crickets, but he had lost visual contact with his four pals.

He could feel his heart hammering much as it did every year on the first day of football practice, and for the first time that night began to regret his decision to join the others in sneaking on to the golf course "What am I doing here?" he thought. "This is crazy, man." Then he heard Johnson utter in a horse whisper, "Okay! Hubba hubba. Let's go for broke. Full speed ahead. Damn the torpedoes. John Wayne would be proud of us!"

"What's John Wayne got to do with this?" grumbled Kingfisher who was crouching alongside Johnson in the gloom to Perry's left. "I don't think he even plays golf."

"Yes, he does," growled Williams from in back of them. "I saw it in *Life Magazine*. He was playing with Bing Crosby. So shut up. This is no time to chicken out. In a minute I'll have my hands on our first flag. No sweat."

"What hole are we assaulting in this nefarious maneuver? squeaked Sherwood from somewhere behind the others.

"It doesn't matter, Einstein," hissed Perry, and he began to sprint across the soft cushion of nicely mowed grass. He ran easily, feeling weightless, simply floating over the fairway like some ghostly phantom. Ahead he thought he could barely make out their target, which happened to be the 14th green complete with fluttering flag. On all sides he could hear the muffled footfalls of his four companions. Or, at least he thought all four were running. You could never be certain about Sherwood.

Williams, always the swiftest, was the first to reach the manicured grass of the green. Without breaking stride, he accelerated, and reached out with his right hand for the flapping flag on the skinny pole. Snaapp! The top one-third of the pole broke off leaving a jagged spire pointing skyward. "Oops!" shouted Williams, as he plunged down the slope behind the green.

"Oh, no!" shrieked Sherwood. "That's too licentious. Now we're deadsville!"

"Quit whining," barked Perry. "Ohhh, crap!" The ground suddenly fell away beneath him, and he pitched forward, out of control. He landed softly on his shoulder, but when he reached out a hand, he couldn't feel any grass. It felt gritty. Then it made sense. He was in a sand trap. "Why did I ever think this was going to be a cinch?" he mumbled as he brushed granules from his sweatshirt.

—◦◦◦—

It had all begun innocently enough. They hadn't planned to get together, but one by one, the quintet had shown up at their favorite meeting place, Williams' basement, or rather half-basement. Williams' parents had purchased the 1940's bungalow with the idea of digging out a full basement, but never got around to completing the task. As a result, only a portion of the space—the part occupied by Williams' bed, nightstand, four-drawer bureau, a couple of chairs and assorted clutter—was livable. The wall on the far end behind the oil burning furnace consisted of musty-smelling, packed earth. Cobwebs hung from the rafters of the unfinished ceiling. The entire place was dimly lit, and it looked more like some untidy animal's den than a bedroom.

But to the five assembled members of New Rose High School's 1955 Senior Class, it seemed just right——far better than anything that their mothers might drool over in the pages of *Good Housekeeping*.

Perry Palmer sat backwards on a paint-splattered wooden chair and happily surveyed the scene. He had known the others since early in elementary school, and felt more comfortable with them than with his biological family. Unlike the rest, he was fatherless, and because he frequently was at odds with his widowed mother, he preferred to spend as much time as possible in the homes of his friends.

Perry was the only one wearing glasses, and the thick black frames gave his round face an owlish look. Shorter than the rest, and squarish in build, he was the most awkward of the bunch, constantly knocking things off tables and bumping into people. When he smiled, he tried to hide his slightly crooked teeth, and silently he begrudged his mother's unwillingness to pay for braces. Even though he knew it was probably unrealistic, he still hoped he might grow a few inches taller so he would have a chance to make the basketball team.

The five all lived in modest, one-bathroom houses in the same neighborhood. The fathers worked for the railroad, for the aluminum plant, for an auto parts distributor, and for the city. Among the moms, only Perry's worked outside the home. Nobody's parents had ever been divorced. It wasn't quite a Norman Rockwell painting of Middle America, but it was close.

Despite their common background, similar Anglo-Saxon names, and shared interests, they possessed significantly different personalities and looks. That was what Perry found so appealing. They were all so much the same, and yet all so different. Not like his family, which was all the same, period.

Perry was further pleased to note that everyone assembled was in his favorite spot in the basement: Perry on the old chair, Danny Williams squatting cross-legged on his unmade bed, Randy Sherwood leafing through a pile of old *National Geographics*, Ray Kingfisher sitting on the wooden staircase, and Ron Johnson pacing like a caged bear.

It was Johnson who broke the momentary silence: "It's ree-diculous," he snarled. "Summer's almost over, and we haven't done anything worth doing. He pointed at William's Big Ben alarm clock. *"The minutes of our lives are ticking away!* We'll be stone cold dead before anything interesting happens."

"Boy, if that isn't just like Johnson," Perry thought, "never satisfied." He scanned the dingy room and smiled to himself. Williams' basement had been Perry's favorite space since the seventh grade. He surveyed the dusty clutter with envy: *Mad* magazines piled by the unmade bed, a rickety night-stand barely large enough for the alarm clock and a 45 rpm record player, an array of 45 platters spilling across the floor. It was such a contrast to his house where every stick of furniture was lemon-polished, every inch of linoleum Johnson-waxed, every doily placed just so on the overstuffed chairs. He also felt warmer here. Even since his mother had changed the furnace from sawdust to an oil burner, their house always seemed chilly. He looked up and suddenly realized Johnson was expecting him to say something

"So, got any ideas?" asked Perry.

"I'm counting on our lazy buddy for inspiration," barked Johnson, pointing across the room at Williams. It was mid-day, but Williams was still in his wrinkled pajamas. Cartoon knights in armor rode up his arms and across his back. Scattered on the fabric were the words, "Once a Knight!" Last year he had worn the top to the Sadie Hawkins dance.

"Don't look at me," he said. "Sherwood's the guy with all the brains."

Sherwood put the magazine down and stuck his hands in his cords. "Why pick on me? Kingfisher is unquestionably the omniscient guy around here."

"Om what?" shouted Williams. "Speak English, for crying out loud."

"I can't help it if you are a congenital ignoramus," replied Sherwood whose fondness for long words frequently irritated his friends.

Kingfisher was leaning against the stair rail and yawning. After a long pause, he said, "What's wrong with just hanging out?"

"It's dumb, that's what," replied Johnson. "We only got so many good days on this planet, and we've got to make them count. Tomorrow you might get hit by a bus."

"Hey, good idea," shouted Sherwood. "Let's see if we can get a bus to obliterate Kingfisher."

"We could shoot some hoops in Johnson's backyard," offered Perry.

"No, we couldn't," said Johnson. "Remember what happened last time? You insisted on shooting those long jumpers and the ball kept landing on my mom's prize zinnias. I've been told if that happens again I'm grounded for a month."

"What a bunch of geniuses," said Williams. "You guys have fewer ideas than the average spastic."

"How about playing some golf?" said Kingfisher, staring up at a mass of dusty cobwebs. At his father's urging, he had taken up the game a few years back, and this summer had talked Williams and Johnson into playing a couple of rounds at the New Rose nine-hole course. Perry recalled hitting a bucket of balls with him at the adjoining driving range.

"Too expensive, too ostentatious," said Sherwood, who in addition to being the least adventurous of the group, was also its resident tightwad.

"Plus you need clubs," said Johnson.

"There is a way to keep it cheap," suggested Perry. "How about miniature golf? Then all you need are some putters." Downtown New Rose boasted an elaborate "garden golf" course that dated back to the 30's. Players used ancient putters to poke balls through tunnels, around blind corners, and up slanted ramps. A free game was awarded for any holes-in-one, which rarely happened. It was considered a pretty good place to take a date because the girls giggled a lot and relished the chance to play better than the boys.

"Still too many zlotys," said Sherwood who remembered reading a newspaper story about the currency problems in Poland.

"Wait a minute," shouted Williams jumping off his bed. "Why don't we build our own miniature course? Perry's got the ground. He must have half an acre back of his house by the old chicken coop. There's room for six holes for sure and maybe a full nine if we put in a couple of doglegs under the Gravenstein trees."

Perry shook his head in disbelief. "It'll never work. And besides, this is going to make our lives more interesting?"

Williams stuck a finger in Perry's face. "Wake up. If we do this right, it could be a cheap date. We could rig up some lights and brag to the girls about how creative we are. Who knows, maybe some day we'll be on the cover of *Look* as famous golf course architects."

Kingfisher nodded approval. "Right. And even with a few light bulbs it would be plenty dark, so we'd have an excellent chance of getting some healthy smooching in. And I can easily scrounge up some clubs. What do you think, Perry? During the day we could even charge admission to the fifth and sixth graders who live nearby."

Perry shrugged. "Fine, as long as we figure out a way to sneak the dates back there without my mom catching on. She goes to bed so early, we might be able to pull it off." He smiled. "If we build this thing, I'll have to convince her that miniature golf is nothing but good, clean fun."

"Flags!" exclaimed Williams. "We got to have flags to mark the holes." He glared at Johnson. "I mean the real McCoys from real live golf courses."

"You know, that's totally stupid," snapped Sherwood. "It's completely lacking in sagacity."

"No, it's not 'lacking in sagassatzy'," retorted Johnson "It just so happens I know how to get all those flags for free." They're just waiting for us at Glendoveer."

There was a moment of collective silence. Perry knew that Glendoveer was the largest public golf course in the area, and was surrounded by a eight-foot-high cyclone fence. Obviously, the guys who ran the place wouldn't smile at the idea of a bunch of high school kids waltzing around nabbing their flags.

"So Glendoveer's going to be magnanimous and donate them to us out of the goodness of their pointy little heads?" Sherwood rolled his eyes.

"Of course not, doofus. We'll just have to hijack some." Johnson smiled confidently.

"Oh, great," moaned Sherwood tossing his *National Geographic* at Johnson's head. "We'll just confiscate them right in front of a bunch of big, hairy mendacious golfers? Fat chance!"

"No, no, no," answered Johnson rubbing his hands together. "We'll harvest those babies at night in glorious pitch-black darkness, and nobody will be the wiser.

"Hey, not bad" shouted Williams.

"Those lunkheads at Glendoveer will wake up, see all those missing flags, and think they've been hit in the wazoo by ghosts. They won't have a clue."

The heady scent of outrageous action was now penetrating the moldy basement air. The quintet inhaled deeply.

"Beats just hanging around picking our navels," declared Johnson.

"Count me in," said Kingfisher.

"Me, too," echoed Williams.

"Why not?" said Perry, although at the same time he was thinking, "Ooh, baby, this could be trouble."

"I don't know," said Sherwood. "What's so great about miniature golf anyway? Besides, what happens if we get apprehended?

Williams picked up a dirty white tennis ball from the floor and fired it at Sherwood's head. "For cripes sake, don't be so cotton-picking square. This is a golden opportunity to finally do something that isn't boring. Nobody's going to catch us. I say, let's hit Glendoveer as soon as it gets good and dark." Four heads nodded in silent agreement. Sherwood just shrugged.

The die was cast, and that evening found all five, including a reluctant Sherwood, in dark clothes and mud-streaked faces, slithering alongside Glendoveer's steel fence. It was a warm, star-flecked night with no moon showing, and the resident crickets were in full voice. Johnson earlier had discovered a gaping hole in the barrier. "Some drunk crashed through it in a big, old pickup," he explained, "and I guess they've never got around to patching it up."

With 36 holes Glendoveer was the most-used public golf course for miles around, an oasis of well-tended greenery with a huge colonial-style clubhouse. Kingfisher, who had walked the course a couple of times with his dad, was the only one with any knowledge of the terrain. To the others, it was foreign territory even in daylight. At night it loomed as a shadowy, forbidden planet, complete with hidden bunkers as Perry soon discovered.

"Are you okay?" asked Kingfisher peering down at Perry. "Did you break anything?"

"Shut up, and help me find where Williams went," replied Perry. He fumbled around in the sand and retrieved his glasses.

"He's over there under that big oak tree with the other guys. Come on, let's decide which hole we hit next." Kingfisher sounded elated, almost giddy.

Once they had all assembled under the leafy limbs of the huge tree, Johnson was the first to see the spots of light. Then Williams noticed them as well. "Nuts!" he hissed. "They've got to be flashlights. But why?"

"What lights?" asked Perry trying to make out where they were pointing.

"OhmyGod," whispered Sherwood. "It's the gendarmes. They've been tipped off. They're just waiting to annihilate us. My dad's going to kill me."

"Wait a minute," murmured Perry. "That can't be. What would cops be doing on this golf course? Williams, you're the fastest. Sneak up there, and see what's going on." Williams uttered a muffled protest and then darted into the darkness. In spite of his confident order to Williams, Perry wondered what the lights did mean. If Williams didn't return quickly, Sherwood was apt to bolt for the hole in the fence.

Agonizing minutes passed. Well before anyone could see him, Williams could be heard, running hard. When his shape finally materialized, it startled Perry. It was as though Williams had suddenly been sprung from the earth's bowels, a rumpled, slightly winded spook.

"Nightcrawlers," he announced in a hoarse whisper.

"What?" demanded Johnson.

"Nightcrawlers, you dork! Those flashlights are guys busy pulling up worms. They're aren't cops. They're fishermen looking for bait."

Sherwood grabbed Perry's arm. "It's still too close for comfort. Let's vamoose before anybody can identify our physiques."

Perry punched Sherwood lightly in the ribs. "Quit blubbering, Sherwood. They can't see us over here. We might as well get some more flags."

"Now, you're talking," agreed Johnson.

"I hear you," said Williams, who suddenly turned and began sprinting toward what he guessed was the 15th green.

The four others took out after him, and Kingfisher immediately lost his footing on the wet grass and slid, laughing, into the edge of the rough. Sherwood was behind him and still grumbling. "We gotta get outta here. They're going to stick us with destroying private property! It'll be *habeas corpus*, and we'll be incarcerated for sure."

Perry wondered if Sherwood knew what he was talking about. He wished Williams had been a little more careful. Once again he was nearly blind in the darkness.

"Dadrat it, Sherwood, don't go belly up on us now," said Perry in a low voice. "Get the lead out and help me find that idiot, Williams."

Perry smiled to himself. This whole evening seemed unreal, starting with the story he had cooked up for his mother who now thought he was spending the night at Kingfisher's. He wondered how she would react if she ever found out he and his friends had spent an evening pirating golf flags. Most likely she simply would refuse to believe it. Tomorrow he'd have to come up with some plausible story to explain why he and his buddies were about to spend an unusual amount of time with rakes and shovels in her backyard. Oh well, he'd worry about that later. Right now he had to concentrate on finding Williams who was somewhere ahead, madly churning toward the 15th green.

Chapter Two
The Hermits Club

Progress on the miniature golf course was not going well. The nocturnal raid on Glendoveer had produced six flags, which now were stored in the old chicken house on the back of Perry's property. But once the excitement of the flag heist began to wear off, so did the enthusiasm for the construction effort.

Perry's folks had purchased the rectangular half-acre in 1931 and built a shake-sided, two-story house close to the street. The contractor's bill, still wedged in a cubbyhole on the family desk, read, "paid in full $3,605.80." In Perry's early years when his father was still alive, the spacious backyard lawn was crisply mowed and maintained, but more recently had succumbed to a blitzkrieg of broad-leafed weeds. An unruly laurel hedge that screened the chicken house from view partitioned off the back one-third of the lot. Behind this shrubbery, on territory once occupied by a covey of Rhode Island Reds, was the ground where Perry and friends hoped to place their nine miniature holes. The hedge would also keep their project hidden from the prying eyes of any nosy adults.

Perry, Johnson, and Williams spent one overcast Saturday attempting to shovel out the miniature fairways and soon discovered that it was not as simple as they first imagined. Perry's ground was covered with Canadian thistles and crabgrass, and after a heavy shower, turned to mucky gumbo.

Perry's mother briefly visited the site to satisfy her curiosity, and sternly advised the group, "When you start excavating, don't you dare damage the roots of that Gravenstein tree." She was a dumpling-shaped woman who preferred shapeless, floral-patterned house dresses. Streaks of gray were prominent in her dark hair, and Perry was acutely aware that she was older in manner and style than the mothers of his friends.

"You don't have to worry, mom," he assured her. "Any fool can see we won't be digging that deep."

"Well, be sure you don't," she snapped, and, smiling broadly at Williams who was her favorite, she turned and ambled away through the overgrown opening in the hedge.

After her departure, arguments quickly surfaced as to the course's design, which was mostly of Williams' thinking. "Why such a big curve on number three?" wailed Johnson, "and how come you're doing such a lousy job of packing down the dirt? It's all bumpy and crappy-looking. Even Sam Snead couldn't sink a putt on that hole."

"So, snotnose, you're some kind of an expert on golf courses?" Snarled Williams, happy for the opportunity to lean on his shovel. "Maybe you should get off your fat behind and show us how."

"Come on, cool it," implored Perry. "If we keep arguing, we'll never get this thing finished." Johnson kicked a big dirt clod in Williams's direction. "I thought Sherwood and Kingfisher were coming over to help out. How come we're stuck with all the slave labor?"

"How come you're such a lardbutt?" shouted a voice on the other side of the laurel hedge that bordered the chicken house. Slowly Kingfisher came through an opening in the hedge and strutted up to the trio with a sour look on his well-tanned face.

"So, what's eating you?" demanded Perry.

"Women! That's what's wrong with this world. They're absolutely impossible. Especially Pamela Tucker. What a stuck-up airhead." Kingfisher was noted for dating some of the best-looking New Rose coeds, so his lament seemed out of synch with his reputation. With his precisely barbered hair, movie star face, slim build, and perfect tan, he never lacked for female company—a fact that often irritated his dateless friends. He was also the best dresser of the crowd, a marked contrast to the others who preferred to wear the same clothes with monotonous regularity. In May he had been elected student body president for the coming school year, and lately had been acting very full of himself

"Well, you could always turn queer," offered Johnson.

"Or how about becoming a monk?" suggested Williams. "Better yet, a hermit!"

Perry pulled up a thistle and fired it at Kingfisher's head. It sailed wild by several feet. "With our luck with girls lately, we might as well all be hermits. If Kingfisher is having trouble with the fair sex, then the rest of us might as well throw in the towel."

Williams sat down on the steps of the chicken house and wiped a few drops of sweat from his forehead. "For once you're two thousand percent right, Mr. Kingkong. Last night was the end for Shirley and me. We were all set to go to the drive-in and see *On the Waterfront*. But then she said she wanted to see *Dial M for Murder* at the Broadway. So, we got into this stupid argument, and before you could say boo, she announced 'if that's the way you want to be, just forget it! I don't want to go anywhere with somebody as stubborn as you.'"

"Should have offered to take her to *Reefer Madness* at the Blue Mouse," suggested Johnson. "That's the one getting all the headlines."

"Yeah, I'm sure that's just what she wanted to hear. Anyhow, she finally says, 'take her home right now,' and the whole evening was a bust, a complete fursluggener bust. I can't wait for that French exchange babe to arrive and show her up."

"What French Exchange Babe?" asked Perry.

Williams scowled. "Perry, why are you always the last to be in the know? It was announced last May, plus there was a story in the *Bud*."

Kingfisher squatted on his haunches and squinted hard at Williams. "What if we showed those dames we didn't need them, that we could care less about dating any of them? That might really put them in their place."

"You mean take some vow like nuns and priests do?" Johnson looked doubtful.

"No, not like that, more along the lines of lodge brothers; like the Knights of Pythias or the Moose. And maybe we could all take an oath or cross our fingers in blood; you know, we'd all pledge to swear off women for the foreseeable future."

"Or, at least until they quit being so stuck-up," suggested Perry. He'd only dated a couple of girls so far and felt he was way behind in knowledge of the so-called fair sex. "But to do it right we should have strict rules like a charter, or a constitution, and everybody would have to sign their John Henrys."

"Count me in," declared Williams. "Although maybe we should make an exception for the French dish, if she really is a dish."

"Me, too," echoed Johnson, "but there can't be any exceptions. And we know Sherwood will go for this. He doesn't date hardly anybody to begin with. He's already a perfect fit for our plan."

Kingfisher stood up and spread his arms wide. "Okay, so who's going to write up the rules so we make this official?"

"I nominate Mr. P. Palmer," proclaimed Johnson.

"I agree so it's unanimous," pronounced Kingfisher. "Congratulations, Perry, when can we expect the first draft?"

"Wait a minute," shouted Williams. "It is not unanimous. I didn't get a chance to vote."

Kingfisher shrugged. "So, you're out of luck. You don't want the job, do you?"

"Absolutely not, but it's a matter of principle: you know, my voting rights. To set the record straight I also cast my ballot for the Palmer nomination."

"Geez, talk about being railroaded," groused Perry. But beneath his surface scowl, he was pleased. While the other guys were big on math, his favorite class was English. This summer he had read Hemingway's *For Whom the Bell Tolls*, and thought it was terrific. Now he would have a chance to pen something original even if it didn't qualify as The Great American Novel.

"Give me a week or so, and I'll see what I can come up with."

The following Saturday afternoon found all five charter members of the New Rose Anti-Date Consortium huddled in Williams' basement. Originally this was to be a workday on the miniature golf course, but all welcomed an excuse to put off the manual labor. Perry passed out carbon copies of his brainstorm.

"I think 'Hermits' is the best choice for an ordinary name, he said, "but to add some class I rooted through my Winston Dictionary, Advanced Edition, and found a cool-cat synonym: *cenobites*! Thus, we should call our secret society 'CAO' or Cenobites of America Organized."

"Excellent," declared Williams.

"Not bad," agreed Kingfisher.

"I guess it's okay," nodded Johnson.

Sherwood shook his head in disbelief. "Are you sure that's the right word? Cenobite sounds like some kind of hairy-legged insect."

"According to my dictionary it means 'a close-knit religious order,'" said Perry. "That's close enough, so shut up and quit nit-picking. This constitution rivals anything Thomas Jefferson could put out even if Alexander Hamilton was sharpening his pencils. I've covered everything: creed, objectives, secret sign, slogan. All that's missing is a national anthem. If you'll shut your yaps, I'll read aloud this historic document:

"The Constitution of the Cenobites of America Organized, or CAO. Also known as The Hermits." He cleared his throat. "PREAMBLE! We, the select and enlightened male members of the New Rose USA community, do, with the grace of God and in a state of sound mind and body, amalgamate in the Year of Our Lord 1954, AD to form an able-functioning, semi-enduring organization with the illustrious full and recognized name of Cenobites of America Organized, or The Hermits."

"Wow," said Johnson. "Aren't you laying it on pretty thick?"

"Shut up," said Perry. "It just gets better and better." He again cleared his throat.

"Article one—purpose and paraphernalia. Objective: The idea behind the formation of this invincible group is to create an amiable male social club whose main purpose is to have fun and frolic without the involvement/association of the female species."

"Amen, brother," shouted Williams.

Perry resumed his oration. "The Secret Sign! The accepted and recognized sign of CAO is the placing of the shortest and thickest digit of the human hand, i.c. the pollex or thumb, immediately alongside the facial organ housing the external olfactory organs, *i.e.* the nose. This sign should be given whenever CAO members sight each other anywhere in the civilized world."

"Just as along as it doesn't look like we're picking boogers," interrupted Johnson.

"Only a complete, four-eyed moron like you would think that," retorted Perry. He continued on:

"Slogan. The acknowledged slogan of CAO is the concise, far reaching and abundantly meaningful phrase, 'So What!'

"Article two, the meeting place: All regular, legitimate meetings of CAO are to be held in a vehicle manufactured for road travel which is moved by a source of power within itself, *i.e.* a car. Instances where urgency warrants it, meetings may be held elsewhere but only in the case of a supreme emergency."

"Hold on," shouted Sherwood. "Some of us don't have cars at our beck and call."

"Yeah, but Perry and I do, and the rest of you can borrow your parents' machines most of the time," countered Johnson. "Don't be a knucklehead."

Perry turned to his last page and recited:

"Article three. Membership: CAO has been formed to be an intimate, somewhat exclusive organization whose members must cease, desist and refrain from the unhermitable practice of dating New Rose damsels. Note: no exceptions for foreign exchange students.

"Article four—crime and punishment: A black and dire crime against CAO shall occur if any member willfully disobeys or disregards the provisions of this *excruciatingly* clever and well-written constitution. Penalties imposed shall be as following, depending on the magnitude of the devious malfeasance: One— Expulsion from the group. Two— Suspension for a specified time, followed by parole. Three—A suitable, harsh reprimand from the highest officer. Four— Being paraded by members in good standing in front of the front row of cars at the Jim Dandy Drive-In. Five— Having to dance with Eunice 'Hogbreath' Schultz for two full songs at the New Rose High School noon dance."

"Oooh, that's a good one," said Williams.

"Hang on, I'm almost finished," said Perry. "Article Five: Offices and officers. Officers of CAO are selected by the membership based on hermitive qualifications and background. The person judged most hermitive will be the highest officer, followed by the next most hermitive, on down to the least hermitive. Because of the uniqueness of CAO, *every* member shall hold an office of some kind. I suggest the following lineup of officers for our startup period: *Supreme Superlative Sovereign*: Randolph Franklin Sherwood. *Prolific Philosophical Potentate*: Perry Alexander Palmer. *Magnanimous Majestic Maharajah*: Ronald Martin Johnson. *Imperial Awe-inspiring Grand Duke*: Daniel Marshall Williams. *Sanguinary Savage Czar*: Raymond Frederick Kingfisher."

There was a moment of collective silence.

"So, what do you think?" proudly asked Perry.

"Actually not bad," said Johnson.

"Groovy," said Williams

"A doozy," said Kingfisher

"Are you sure that's the way to spell 'excruciatingly?'" asked Sherwood staring quizzically at his carbon copy.

Chapter Three
Real Estate Signs

Summer was nearly over, and the newly minted Hermits were in a funk. Interest in the miniature golf course was lagging, and it was another week before football practice would commence. The no-date policy was still in effect, but already there were signs of mutiny. There was a general unanswered longing for ferment, turmoil, commotion—anything that would dispel the doldrums before school started again. "Our lives are like molasses in low gear," complained Johnson.

The miniature golf course project was suffering, not only from indifferent spade work, but also by the arrival of a mole family. It had established living quarters on two of the proposed putting greens, and each time the earth was smoothed and packed down enough to allow a golf ball to roll decently, the moles would proceed to push up a cluster of mini-Matterhorns. Clouds of discourage-ment piled up on the Hermits' horizons.

Jammed into Johnson's parked 1941 Ford coupe, the quintet considered their options. The car, given to Johnson by his grandfather, was prized for its 85 horsepower V-8 engine. It had been lovingly polished on the exterior but showed signs of hard use inside. Johnson was eating an apple, and Perry, stuck in the middle of the soft back seat, was intrigued by his friend's unusual technique. Johnson was the only person Perry had ever known who would devour an apple completely, including skin, core and seeds.

Johnson, like the others, was several inches taller than Perry, and possessed darker hair and heavy eyebrows. The edge of his round face was peppered with eruptions of acne. Slightly older than the others, he had been the first to get a driver's license and the first to nail down a good-paying summer job at the Dairy Queen. He considered himself "to be a man of action," and his friends acknowledged that he was rarely calm. In junior high, classmates had called him "Ex-Lax," because he was always chanting, "Let's go! Let's go!"

Sherwood, sitting on Perry's right side, was, as usual, looking worried, and he cleared his throat loudly before speaking: "If we're not going to finish the golf course, maybe we should at least return all those golf flags we pinched. You know, get rid of the incriminating evidence that's stashed in Perry's chicken house."

Sherwood was tall, skinny, taciturn, and the most serious and studious of the bunch. In classes like chemistry and advanced math, he breezed through experiments and tests with disgusting ease—attracting the praise and knowing smiles of teacher after teacher. Proud of his expanding vocabulary, he loved to irritate others by using polysyllable words. With his high forehead and long, solemn face, he was occasionally called "Platy," the result of a sophomore biology class when Arnie Fitzroy looked up from his microscope and yelled, "Hey, Sherwood's face looks just like *platyhelminthes*, you know, the flatworm."

"For cripes sakes, Sherwood, you are the original party pooper. That is the dumbest thing I've heard from you in at least the last five minutes," retorted Williams who was wedged in on the other side of Perry. "We sweated bullets to get those flags, and we sure as Shinola aren't going to just hand them back."

Perry wiggled to sit up straight. "Wait a minute," he said, "Maybe we don't give them back, but instead stick 'em in people's front yards; you know, people we don't like."

"You mean like Beasely?" exclaimed Johnson. Barclay Beasely was the New Rose principal and about as popular as chicken pox.

"None other," replied Perry.

"Beats just twiddling our thumbs," said Kingfisher pulling his foot out of the window.

"Good grief," moaned Sherwood. "That scenario would get us expelled for sure."

"Platy, quit being a pussycat," snarled Williams. "This could be great. We slip out tonight and stick them in his front yard where everybody passing by would wonder how they got there. People might even think he took 'em for souvenirs." He warmed to his subject. "He'd never know what hit him, and he would be totally pee-ood."

"But, geez, we only got six flags total. That will hardly make a big splash." It was Sherwood, the cool head. "And we're sure not going to jeopardize our livers to confiscate more."

"Okay, okay, fair enough," said Williams, "We'll keep the flags for trophies, but then what the crud should we use? Flaming crosses like the Klu Klux Klan?"

"I got it," exclaimed Perry. "For sale signs!"

"For what?" Johnson turned around so abruptly his elbow hit the horn ring.

"You know, real estate signs. 'For Sale by Snodgrass Realty' or whatever. They're all over the place. We just pull up a trunk-full and then stick them like tombstones in Beasely's yard."

"That's got potential," said Kingfisher. "Old Beaser-head might get the hint that lots of people would like to see him sell out and move on." He paused and fiddled with the sun visor. "Plus, maybe we could plant some on the lawns of those conceited senior girls."

"Yeah! like Shirley Gadrather," agreed Williams who was still seething that Shirley had dumped him. "Then she might wake up and realize we Hermits have to be taken seriously."

"And Amy Quinton," shouted Johnson. Amy was Pep Club president and generally regarded as impossibly stuck-up.

"I could finally get sweet revenge on Pamela Tucker," chimed in Kingfisher.

"At least if we got arrested, it probably would only be a misdemeanor," said Sherwood. "Especially if we forget the golf flags."

"Let's do it," bellowed Johnson. "We can go scout up some signs right now." He started the Ford and peered at the instrument panel. Then he took his index finger and tapped one of the gauges. "Anybody got a couple of bucks for gas? It's gone up to 35 cents a gallon, for pete's sake."

Collecting the signs proved to be relatively simple. Two new subdivisions were under construction near the high school, and for sale signs dotted many of the cramped front lawns. That afternoon found Johnson repeatedly parking the Ford with the motor running while one of his cohorts spilled out, and on the dead run, yanked the sign free of the ground. Sprinting back to the car, he opened the trunk, tossed in the sign and dove into the front seat.

"How many we got now?" asked Johnson as he slam-shifted into second gear.

"A couple dozen, easy," said Williams.

"Actually, we now have nineteen," said Sherwood. "I've been mathematically calculating a tally on the palm of my hand."

Johnson turned down Sandy Avenue and stuck his elbow out the driver's side window. "I think we only need a couple more to do the job," he said. "And I propose to show you guys how a real professional sign burglar does it." A barrage of catcalls greeted him from all sides.

"Baloney."

"Crappola."

"Big talk."

"Come on! Be sagacious. Let's quit while we're ahead."

Johnson made a left turn on Maywood Drive. The Maywood Park neighborhood was the most upscale in New Rose. The houses were larger, sat on bigger lots and had more attractive landscaping. "Just you watch. I'll show you how Humphrey Bogart or the Green Hornet would do this."

He abruptly pulled into the driveway of a two-story Cape Cod dwelling. A red and blue sign in the middle of the lawn proclaimed:

FOR SALE
by Premium Properties
call Stan Quackenbush, realtor,
AL 3-8778

A heavyset man wearing a checkered shirt and owlish glasses was watering his flowerbed with a garden hose. He turned to see who was in his driveway. Johnson put the Ford in neutral and set the hand brake. Then he bounded out of the car and swaggered up to the sign.

"Good Morning," he boomed out to the man, and saluting with his right fingers, he deftly uprooted the sign with his left hand. "Nice day, eh?" He strolled back to the car and tossed the sign to a startled Williams in the shotgun seat. The older man's mouth dropped, and he momentarily hosed the side of his house.

"Made in the shade," bragged Johnson as he released the brake and backed out smoothly. Then he abruptly goosed the accelerator, popped the clutch and squealed away.

"Now, that, my pointy-headed friends," said Johnson smugly, "is how the pros swipe signs—with class and brass. Upon observing my technique the Green Hornet would be green alright, green with envy!"

There was muttered approval from throughout the Ford, and then Williams piped up, "Okay, okay. Big deal. Now let's get a few more, and then we got to decide where we're going to plant these babies."

"Whatever we do, let's not push our luck too far," pleaded Sherwood. "We don't want to turn into kleptomaniacs." For emphasis, he leaned over Perry and stuck a fist in Williams' face.

"Hey, who cut the cheese?" yelled Williams holding his nose with two fingers.

Chapter Four
Football Practice

The end of August signaled the end of listless days for those at New Rose H.S. who considered themselves, more or less, to be athletes. It meant the start of football practice for the Thorns, commencing with the dreaded daily double workouts which were always scheduled the week before school officially began. Now that all the real estate signs had been stuck in appropriate yards, Perry felt it was indeed time to be serious about something. He was relieved to hear that the sheriff wasn't interested in pursuing Principal Beasely's complaint about the half dozen for sale signs stuck in his lawn. Most of the senior girls had shrugged off the episode as well, although Pamela Tucker's father had threatened to "boil in oil" those responsible.

It was a glorious time for Williams who was legitimately a football player of some note. He was the Thorn's fastest back, an elusive, slippery gazelle who charmed coaches and cheerleaders alike. Slim and sinewy, he was the best athlete of the group, a natural at all sports who laughed often and easily, whether he was winning or losing. Unlike most males in the class of '55 he chose not to crewcut his hair brutally short in the dominant style of the times. Instead he combed the front high and was trying to cultivate sideburns. Williams' hands were unusually large and his long fingers were perfect for gripping the seams of a baseball or snaring an errant forward pass.

His cohorts were hardly the stuff of Grange and Nagurski. Perry at 5'-5," weighed 155 somewhat flabby pounds, and while he probably would start at left offensive guard, he was prone to avoiding serious contact. Instead he prided himself on "finesse blocking" which generally meant falling down and attempting to trip any opponent over 200 pounds.

Kingfisher had turned out primarily to please his dad and was even more lacking in ferocity than Perry. For reasons that baffled his teammates, the coaches had indicated they wanted him to center for punts and extra points.

Johnson was a clod-footed halfback who played with reckless abandon but was so prone to fumbling that he rarely was given a chance to carry the ball. He was widely admired for his talent at slipping analgesic balm into the jock straps of showering JV players.

Sherwood had suffered a broken rib as a freshman defensive back and ever since his parents had insisted he concentrate on basketball. During football season he kept statistics for the team.

Fortunately for all of them, New Rose H.S. was a far cry from a gridiron powerhouse. If the Thorns won more than three games a season, it was considered a banner year. Fewer than 30 boys annually tried out for the varsity squad, and by mid-season, injuries and drop-outs cut the numbers down so severely that it was hard to field two complete teams to scrimmage. Some of the injuries were directly related to the Thorn's dismal practice field which was bulldozed out of a rocky hillside when the high school was constructed. Grass grew only in sorry patches on the thick clay soil, and rocks, sometimes the size of hand grenades, continued to work up through the surface. Thorn players prayed for the first heavy rains of fall to soften their landings, but then they were confronted with mud the consistency of 90W gear oil. (Having only the most primitive laundry system, New Rose asked players to wash their own practice uniforms on weekends, causing mild cardiac arrest among players' mothers once they saw the muddy gear defiling their beloved Maytags.)

"This year's going to be different," declared Williams from the shotgun seat of the '40 Chev coupe, as Perry drove to the first day's workout. It was the Palmer family car, but because Perry's mother didn't drive, he had full use of it after his dad died. Perry had attempted to jazz it up a bit with new seatcovers, fake white white tire rims, a glasspack muffler and a chrome extension on the exhaust pipe, but it remained clearly your ordinary, everyday small Chevy. The gearshift lever was mounted on the steering column ("three on a tree instead of four on the floor" according to Williams), and Perry had been told that made for easy slam-shifting in a drag situation. However he had never tried the technique as he worried he'd either burn out the clutch or drop the transmission.

"Says who?" snorted Perry.

"Says me, that's who. Haven't you heard about Mr. McIntyre, the new assistant coach?"

"Only rumors. Kingfisher claimed he was backup for some all-star at the University of Washington."

"Egg-zactly, my man. He was right behind non-other than Archie McBride, the best running back in the Pacific Conference and maybe the world."

Perry down-shifted into the New Rose parking lot and slid to a stop in the gravel. "Well, that doesn't mean a hill of beans to guys like me who do the gruntwork in the line. Plus, we still got Central Catholic on the schedule."

Williams rolled his eyes in mock dismay. "Perry, old buddy, where's your team spirit? If this guy improves our backfield, you guys in the line will have it twice as easy 'cause you won't have to open up such gigantic holes."

"Since when did we ever open gigantic holes anyway!" Perry shook his head. "Plus, let's face the fact that we still got Old Man Gunderson as head coach. He's so old fashioned he doesn't think the T-formation is here to stay."

Williams pounded Perry on the back. "Just wait, my friend. You'll see. We might even get that French exchange cutie on the rally squad. This year could be the start of something big."

"Yeah, like a big lead balloon."

A week later, Perry had to admit the new coach was a breath of fresh air. Mr. McIntyre was a big, good-looking guy with curly hair, bulging biceps and a toothy smile. Unlike silver-haired Coach Gunderson who might watch practice from his DeSoto if it rained too hard, this McIntyre got right in the thick of scrimmages and actually ran some plays, daring the young Thorns to tackle him. And he paid attention to the bumbling linemen, showing them some new blocking angles favored by his Alma Mater.

Practices, however, in the collective opinion of the Thorns, continued to be regarded as only slightly better than medieval torture.

The coaches' favorite penalty for poor performance was to command the offenders to run a lap at full speed around the entire practice field. For huffing, puffing, Perry and his fellow linemen this was in the words of tackle Vernon Grover, "worse than kissing a pig's rear end." In fact, Thurman Barnes, a transfer from Grant High, finally got so fed up running laps he ran right off the field into the dressing room, threw his jersey and pads into the shower and quit the squad on the spot. "It's no big loss," said Williams. "That guy would have been cut for smoking anyhow."

Finally the Friday arrived for the last afternoon of twice-a-day practices, and the staging of the first full-bore intra-squad scrimmage. Williams, as usual, was elated. Playing on the "A" team, he repeatedly broke free for long runs, much to the grousing of Perry and Johnson who were relegated to the "B" group. Kingfisher was nursing a knee injury of undetermined origin and lounged happily on the sidelines.

"Come on, you pansies!" rasped Coach Gunderson as the B's sloppy tackling allowed Williams once again to slither past sprawling defensive linemen and race into the end zone. "If you birdbrains don't figure out a way to play some defense and then actually score some points, you'll be running laps until the cows come home."

"This is ridiculous," wheezed Oliver Hill who played tackle next to Perry. We'll be out here 'til midnight the way things are going."

"Pray for a miracle," muttered Perry.

The A's kicked off and Ernest Funkhouser, the B's fullback, picked up the ball as it bounced through a mud puddle and promptly fumbled it back to the A's.

Coach McIntyre wiped off the slippery pigskin and placed it at midfield. Then he turned and glared at the downcast B's. "Okay, here's my challenge: if you morons get the ball back and score, I'll buy all of you a milkshake at Jim Dandy's. Otherwise you can run a few more laps for Mr. Gunderson."

"Geez, coach," whined Oliver Hill, "we got only 10 guys now on our B team. No wonder we're having problems."

Coach McIntyre glanced over at the sidelines. "For once you're right, Oliver," he said. "Kingfisher! Get off your duff and get in here at linebacker!"

Kingfisher looked as if he had been struck by lightning.

"But, coach, my knee..."

"Hogwash," said the B's other tackle, Vernon Grover. "We're dead meat."

The A's lined up quickly and tried a quarterback sneak. Grove and Hill for once guessed right and stopped the play for no gain. On second down the A's centered the ball to Williams who ran frantically to his right, looking as though he was trying some kind of sweep. Perry, Grover and Hill, all puffing like water buffalo, pursued him. Suddenly Williams stopped, gripped the ball tightly and raised his arm to pass. Downfield, way behind Johnson and the B's other defensive backs, was Arne Larsen, the A's tight end. Williams took a quick step forward and just as he started to throw, turned his ankle on the field's bumpy ground.

The ball slithered sideways, took a crazy bounce off a hidden rock and landed in the hands of the charging Grover who clutched the ball in amazement.

"Fumble!" screamed Perry. "Don't stand there, Grover, RUN!"

"No, lateral, man, lateral!" shouted Johnson, who suddenly appeared on one side. Grover, despite being horsecollared by an A's lineman, underhanded the ball to Johnson who now was in full plow-horse gallop. Breaking into the clear, he was caught by another A's player who attempted to wrestle him to the ground. As he crashed, he desperately flipped the ball back over his head, and into the nervous arms of none other than Kingfisher, who had been primarily concerned with avoiding body contact with any large A's.

"Run, you idiot!" screamed Perry who was busy throwing an illegal crack-back block well away from the main action.

Kingfisher, quickly recognizing that this was a rare chance for football glory, and fervently not wanting to suffer a crushing tackle, ran for his life and dove headfirst across the goal line holding the ball in front of him like an offering to the gods.

The entire B squad reacted as though they had won the Rose Bowl. "Milkshakes!" bellowed Grover, and instantly all voices hollered in unison: "Milkshakes! Milkshakes! Milkshakes!"

Later in the locker room, a smiling Perry snapped a towel at Williams who was rubbing his sore ankle.

"Knock it off," yelled Williams.

"Relax," said Perry. "You just might be right for once. Maybe this year will be different."

September, 1954 News Flashes

Soviet jet fighters down a US Navy Neptune PZV bomber on a patrol mission off the Siberian coast.

Atomic Energy Commission Chairman Lewis Strauss says the US has overwhelming superiority of atomic weapons but warns that Russia might develop a method of delivery against which there is no defense. On September 14, the USSR does test a nuclear weapon.

The last episode of the "Lone Ranger" is broadcast on radio. There were 2,956 episodes aired over 21 years.

Leo Durocher's New York Giants win the National League baseball championship.

★NEW ROSE BUD★

The Student Newspaper of New Rose High School

Vol. XI Number 1   *Friday, September 15, 1954*

(First Edition for the New School Year)

Student Body Pres. Speaks to Students

At the first student body assembly, S. B. President Raymond Kingfisher said, "What is going to make this year one of the most memorable of your life? It will be the effort and cooperation you put into your studies, and your student body activities. So, don't take any wooden nickels!"

He praised the Student Council for amending the New Rose constitution to upgrade golf and tennis from minor to major sports. "About time," said Kingfisher, who happens to be co-captain of the golf team.

French Girl Arrives as Exchange Student

Much interest has been aroused by the news that a charming French girl will be attending our school this year as an exchange student.

She is Francoise Redeaux, and she will be living with Mr. and Mrs. Orville DuPrey Sr. while visiting here. Orville DuPrey Jr. is a well-known senior at our school, and his sister, Orvellene, is a sophomore.

According to Principal B. Beasely, "This is an excellent way to improve relations between our countries, and I expect all students to roll out the welcome mat for Mademoiselle Francoise. Remember how much you like French fries."

Chapter Five
The Milk Spill

The first day of a new school year had always been a mixed bag for Perry, and this year was no exception. Despite being properly attired in brand new Days cords, a Lord Jeff sweater, and white bucks, he felt uneasy about facing his senior year. He was delighted to find he was enrolled in Coach Gunderson's Modern Problems class with its well-served reputation for little or no homework. On the other hand he was bothered to learn he'd been assigned to Mrs. Burkett's advanced math class where only true brains were said to survive. "I'll bet Sherwood is behind this," he thought as he trudged toward his locker at the noon break. "Just because Sherwood loves math, why does he want to rope me in?" he wondered.

Perry, like most of the student body, was rather proud of New Rose High School's up-to-date appearance. Construction had been completed with much hoopla in 1952, and the facility was considerably larger and sleeker than the squat brick building which had previously been the school's home dating back to 1923. The old building had been a boxy, two-story structure, but the new edifice was all one level and sprawled over several acres of a former tomato field. The roofline, said to be "strikingly modern," was completely flat except for the portion over the gym, which loomed whale-like in silhouette. Exterior walls featured large sections of glass block over the windows in the architecturally correct style of the times. Inside, the classrooms were arranged opposite each other and bisected by two lengthy corridors with traditional metal lockers lining the hallways.

Perry's locker was down the school's west corridor and opposite the boy's lavatory. It was well away from the lockers of his buddies, a fact that pleased Perry because of his current lunch sack dilemma. His mother had insisted that he drink milk with lunch and, lacking an ordinary thermos, had elected to provide him with a pint mayonnaise jar of the white stuff. To insure a proper seal she screwed down the lid over a square of waxed paper.

Perry quickly realized that he would be laughed at royally if he showed up with the pint jar at the cafeteria table favored by his friends. "Couldn't I just buy milk like the other guys?" he had pleaded. "Nonsense," she replied. "Why spend money needlessly? Buying milk in gallon jugs is a lot cheaper, and this jar will work just fine." At least she had finally given up trying powdered milk. "Wallpaper paste would taste better," Perry had told her.

From experience he knew how hard it was to change her mind about anything concerning food or drink. For years he had been trying to modify her views about breakfast menus. While his friends were happily munching Wheaties and Rice Crispies, Perry was subjected daily to cooked oatmeal mush. Not only was his mother suspicious of packaged dry cereals, she even had doubts about the nutritional value of Cream of Wheat.

She was also a firm believer in soft-boiled eggs and well-done toast. Actually "well burnt" might be a more apt description due to the design of their ancient toaster. The bread, day-old from the Sun-beam Bakery Thrift Store, rested vertically on hinged trays facing a central, exposed-wire electrical element. Its operation required a keen eye and a steady hand. When it appeared that one side of the bread was suitably singed—or just before black smoke began spilling out—a knob at the bottom of the tray needed to be twisted vigorously. With luck the bread slice would then flop over and be electrically tattooed on the other side. Perry fervently hoped the device would self-destruct one day, but it seemed unbreakable.

On the way to school that morning Perry concocted a plan for dealing with this latest embarrassment. He would dart across the hall into the boy's lavatory, find an empty stall and quickly chug down the milk. Then he could show up at the lunch table with nothing more to defend than the strange, unusually thick sandwiches provided by his mother. If it didn't work, he could always resort to simply dumping the milk in the parking lot before school started.

There was one potential problem: his closest locker neighbors were cheerleader Sandy Smith and Pep Club Prexy Amy Quinton, two of the best-looking girls in the class. Perry thought they looked really cute when they wore their Pendleton skirts and white blouses with Peter Pan collars. Somehow he would have to avoid them.

The morning of the first day proceeded with the normal amount of confusion and griping, until finally the harsh buzzer signaled the arrival of lunchtime. Immediately Perry jumped from his desk and hustled down the hallway toward his distant locker eager to take care of his milk problem. Halfway there, he noted that two girls in rally squad uniforms were pointing and laughing at something in the vicinity of his locker. "Sheesh," he thought. "It's Sandy and Amy."

He stopped beside them, and Sandy gave him a knowing smile. "Well, Perry, it looks like you're keeping a cow in your locker this year."

"Huh?" said Perry. Both Sandy and Amy broke into shrill giggles and pointed at the floor. To Palmer's horror, he saw a large white puddle forming in front of his locker. Milky droplets oozed from the bottom of the door. "Oh, no," he thought, "the jar tipped over and the wax paper didn't seal the lid." His heart sank. These girls would never let him forget this. His mind raced for a suitable answer.

"Looks like milk, doesn't it?" he offered.

"It certainly does," hooted Amy, who was now doubling over in laughter. "We didn't know you were a dairy farmer, Perry."

"Hey, wait a minute. That's not my locker," implored Perry, knowing full well Amy and Sandy would guess it couldn't be anyone else's.

"Baloney, Perry. You've had that locker since you were a sophomore," crowed Sandy.

"No, no, no. Mine's next to it. I think that belongs to one of the transfer kids. Here I'll get some paper towels and clean it up. You girls go on to lunch. I'll handle it."

"Oh, Perry, you're a pill. You can't fool us," howled Amy.

"Yeah, Perry. Nice try," said Sandy. "But we'll gladly let you play janitor and clean this up. Let's go, Amy." She turned down the hall with Amy close beside her.

"Moooo," said Amy over her shoulder.

Perry charged into the boy's lavatory and began ripping off a bundle of paper towels. He sighed loudly. "What a great way to start your senior year," he murmured. He barged out the door and began sopping up the milk. "I guess it could be worse," he thought. "With my luck half the rally squad could have been with Sandy and Amy."

He opened his locker and used the wadded up paper towels to absorb the puddle where the jar had fallen over. Then, holding the offending jar by its thick neck, he bolted back across the hall into the restroom. Leaning against one of the urinals he unscrewed the top of the jar, briefly considered dumping its contents, then started to gulp down the remaining milk.

It was at that precise moment when the door flung open and in charged Mr. Struckworth, the shop teacher and JV wrestling coach. He took one look at Perry with his mayonnaise jar and milk dribbling down his chin, and shook his head. "I thought I'd seen everything, Palmer," he said. "But this takes the cake, pissing and gulping down milk at the same time. I've found kids trying to smoke in here, but you're the first sneaky milk drinker I've ever run into."

Perry let out a long sigh and stared foolishly at Mr. Struckworth who continued to shake his head. "Now it *couldn't* be worse," muttered Perry.

Chapter Six
Francoise

Perry was a few minutes late getting to the cafeteria for lunch, and he couldn't find an empty seat among his cronies. Reluctantly he had to settle for a table occupied only by scrawny Eddie "The Mouse" Fletcher and his overweight friend Monty Carpenter. Perry didn't particularly like this duo, but he didn't dislike them either. They always sat in the back of every class and rarely said a word. The rumor was that The Mouse was pretty smart but too lazy to pull any really good grades.

Monty had the worst case of acne Perry had ever seen. His face was a solid mass of red and bluish swellings doted with occasional pus heads poking up like tiny volcanoes on a moonscape. It was hard to look at Monty without staring. Perry had periodic problems of his own with pimples on this forehead and felt sorry for Monty but thought it best to pretend not to notice. After all, there wasn't anything you could do to cure the stuff, although some guys claimed that making out with girls would help. The problem with that solution was no girl in her right mind would want to make out with a boy who had a face like Monty's.

"How's the food today?" asked Perry He noted that both were slurping down the daily cafeteria special which appeared to consist of wiener wraps, carrot sticks and Jell-O. Although he had finally talked her into buying school lunch milk, Perry's mother was dead set against cafeteria meals. "You can never tell what germs could be lurking in those school kitchens," she said.

"Same old crapola," replied The Mouse. "Better than rat poison."

Perry tried to remember how The Mouse had acquired his nickname.

With his pointed face, beady eyes, big ears and bad teeth, Eddie did somewhat resemble a rodent, but so did several other classmates. "Did he have a pet mouse in grade school?" he wondered.

Monty burped loudly. He looked pleased with himself and pushed aside his empty cafeteria tray. "Hey, did you dig the new French chick?"

"You mean the exchange student?" replied Perry.

"Nobody else," grinned The Mouse. "For once in my life I'm glad I signed up for a foreign language. She has a set of knockers that will curl your toes."

"Built like a brick you-know-what," seconded by Monty. "Viva la France."

Perry chewed his hefty sandwich slowly and pondered the news. There were only two foreign languages offered at New Rose, French and Spanish. Both were taught with embarrassing zest by the heavyset Miss Ringwater. Adults described her as "pleasantly plump." Students were known to refer to her as "Miss Pigwater." Perry and his friends, with the exception of Sherwood, had deliberately avoided taking those classes, considering them a waste of time. "A foreign language is about as useful as an eight-fingered catcher's mitt," Williams had pronounced last summer, and Perry tended to agree with him. In general Miss Ringwater's classes were popular mostly with somber girls partial to horn-rimmed glasses.

"Hey, there she is now," said The Mouse, pointing with a carrot stick.

Across the room Perry saw a cluster of girls taking their empty trays to the cafeteria kitchen. Amy Quinton and Amber Kelly, resplendent in their new, pleated skirts, were talking animatedly with a shorter, dark-haired girl whom Perry had never seen before. Even from his distance he could see that she was very good looking and possessed a dazzling smile behind blazing red, pouty lips. He quickly noted she wore a sweater that was much tighter than those favored by New Rose girls. She definitely was turning heads.

"Put your eyeballs back in their sockets, numbskull, and stop drooling on your peanut butter." The harsh whisper came from Kingfisher who had quietly come up and grabbed Perry's shoulder from behind. He winked at Monty and The Mouse who were picking up their trays.

"I suppose you just signed up for French class," replied Perry.

"Fursluggener right, man. It's parley voo, wee, wee for this kid. By the way, I resign, effective immediately, from the Hermits."

"Yeah, well, it seems all the rats are leaving the sinking ship. Williams and Johnson both quit this morning. There's only Sherwood and me left to carry on."

"Tough shoes, my fine, feathered friend," retorted Kingfisher. "Or as we French scholars like to say, *c'est la vie!*"

Chapter Seven
Date Data

As the first month of the new school year came to its usual loosey-goosey conclusion, Perry found Williams and Johnson chortling over the pages of a small booklet. Perry recognized that it was "Date Data," a pocket-sized brochure proudly produced by the Yearbook staff. In it were supposed to be names, birthdays and phone numbers of the entire student body.

"Oooh boy, Mr. Willits got his tit in the wringer for sure this time," said Williams. "Check this out. It's hot off the press." Johnson grinned and nodded.

"What are your babbling about? replied Perry, who knew that Mr. Willits was the faculty advisor for the yearbook.

"Willits didn't proofread the nicknames that somebody stuck in," smirked Williams. We hear old Beasely was bent out of shape when he saw 'Boozy,' 'One-Punch,' 'Pee,' 'Coon,' and 'Weenie.'"

"Hey, the girls are even better," said Johnson waving the booklet at Perry. How about 'Baby Doll,' 'Dizzy Blonde,' 'Hayseed,'and 'Duncie'? Not to mention 'Tubby' for Heather Breckenridge!" Perry had to smile at that one. Heather was the bespectacled daughter of Superintendent Harley Breckenridge.

"You haven't heard the half of it," said Sherwood, who had just come from the library with a bundle of thick books.

Perry tossed the booklet back to Williams. "What do you mean?"

Sherwood plopped the books on the floor and proceeded to sit on them. "Haven't you heard? A bunch of the phone numbers is all mixed up. It's a classic case of malfeasance. For example, you know

Sandy Smith, the cheerleader? Well, her number was switched with Freida Leiwick's."

"Freida Leiwick!" Perry rolled his eyes. "She's the president of the Chess Club, the one with a mustache."

"Indubitably." Sherwood took a deep breath. "So some of those new guys who transferred here from Hill Military called and thought they were really making time with Sandy when all they were really doing was surprising Freida and delighting her mother."

Perry knew Mrs. Leiwick. She lived in the next block and was always buttonholing his mother and asking why the boys didn't ask Freida for a date. "I can hear her now," he said. "You see, Freida darling, it's just what I told you. I'm delighted these silly boys have finally realized that brains are more important than beauty."

"She's not so delighted anymore," continued Sherwood. "When she discovered the mistake, she called Beasely and threatened to sue the school. 'Cruel and inhuman publishing' she called it. But that's not all. The phone number listed for that punk, Randy Jones, is actually the one for the Little Chapel of the Chimes Funeral Parlor. You remember how Randy got caught shoplifting beer? And how he's always bragging about throwing great parties? Well, now the funeral director's been getting calls asking where the party is, and does he know of any chicks who are hot to trot."

"What do you think will happen to Willits?" asked Johnson.

"I conversed with Mrs. Cascadden in the principal's office," replied Sherwood, "and from what I understand he's agreed to print up corrected copies and apologize all over the place. He's going to give Freida and the Chess Club a full color ad in the Yearbook if her mom calls off the litigation. I guess he'll do the same for the Little Chapel of the Chimes."

"How about the new French Tomato?" asked Perry. Is she listed at all?"

"Not exactly," answered Williams. "But good ol' Orville DuPrey

Jr. is here in black & white, and that's the house she's staying in."

Johnson snickered and said, "Aha, Perry, thinking of dialing up the little Parisian cupcake?"

"Not on your life. I'll leave that stuff up to smooth talkers like Kingfisher. Of course, if she happens to throw herself at me, I'll have to accommodate her."

"Har. Dream on," said Johnson. "If that happens, pigs will fly, and alligators will brush their teeth with Pepsodent."

"Fat chance any of us hayseeds will have a chance to date her," complained Williams. "I heard old man DuPrey has threatened to guillotine any boy who tries to get fresh with her."

Perry punched Sherwood lightly on the shoulder. "This is starting off to be a very interesting year. Very. Very. Very."

October, 1954 News Flashes

Irving Berlin's musical movie White Christmas, starring Bing Crosby and Danny Kaye, opens in New York City.

The communist-supporting Viet Minh take control of North Vietnam.

Marilyn Monroe files for divorce from Joe DiMaggio in Santa Monica, CA. (They were married in January.)

Ernest Hemingway, 55, wins Nobel Prize for literature.

The world's first transistor radio is announced by the Texas Instruments Company.

★ NEW ROSE BUD ★

The Student Newspaper of New Rose High School

Vol. XI, Number 2   *Friday, October 12, 1954*

Sadie Hawkins to Climax Twirp Week

It's coming! October 20-25, that super, stupendous, colossal (for boys and girls, too!) annual Twirp Week.

The Pep Club has put out a set of rules for the week:

Twirp Week Rules!!

1. Girls ask for all dates during Twirp Week.
2. Girls open all doors for boys.
3. Carry their books to class for them.
4. Girls ask boys to dance at the Noon Dance.

Also this wicked warning: Anyone violating these rules will be subject to a ticket given by the Twirp Patrol.

Girls who don't get any Twirp Tickets will be eligible to be crowned Queen Twirpest at the Sadie Hawkins Dance. Wicked warning No. 2: No one will be admitted to the Dance unless they are dressed in true Dogpatch style.

"It'll be a gas," said chairwoman Ermajean Row.

Boys P.E. Classes Present Smoker

A smoker, with boxing, wrestling, horse and rider, and pillow fights, will be given in the gym after school on Friday, Oct.19.

Chapter Eight
Noon Dance Gossip

It was Thursday's lunch break, and Perry had just polished off his leftover pot roast sandwich when Johnson grabbed his elbow.

"Hey, you really ought to check out the noon dance, old buddy." Johnson grinned knowingly.

Perry shook his head slowly. The noon dances were New Rose's daily social highlight. Held in a basement room under the gym and reached via a concrete corridor leading to the locker rooms, they lasted only 30 minutes, but were considered the ultimate place to be seen if you were dating someone or trying to get noticed. The drab, windowless room had all the appeal of a bomb shelter, but the battleship gray concrete floor offered a decent surface for dancing. Music was provided by a compact record player generally manned by a nerdish underclassman. Teachers took turns pulling chaperone duty and generally sat in a corner. Perry was more or less hopeless as a dancer, and his palms sweated so profusely he had difficulty holding his partner's hand. Consequently he rarely attended.

"Oh, I know you aren't big on dancing," said Johnson, "but I urge you if nothing else, to just stand on the sidelines and stare like the rest of the misfits."

"Stare at what?" replied Perry. The last time anything unusual had happened at the noon dance was when Stuart "Speedy" Svenson, whose mother favored egg salad sandwiches, got sick to his stomach and upchucked on the record player.

"Stare at coach McIntyre, that's what," gushed Johnson. "He's supposed to be chaperoning, but he's asking girls to dance, and you ought to see how Amber Kelly snuggles up to him."

Perry looked incredulous. "Coach McIntyre? That sounds crazy. Isn't he married or something?"

"Beats me. All I know is that everybody in home room was buzzing about it yesterday. Becky Aldredge said he was *the most!*" Johnson raised his eyebrows ala Groucho Marx.

"Boy, I wonder if old man Beasely has heard about this. He's not too keen on the whole idea of noon dancing to begin with." Perry stood up and stuffed his shirttail into the back of his cords."I guess I better take a look."

When Perry and Johnson got to the concrete-walled room they could see that it was far more crowded than usual. The number of dancers was about the same as always, but the throng of onlookers was twice its normal size. Williams greeted them by waving his hand over his head.

"Wowser, Coach can cut a mean rug," he said with a smirk.

"He's really asking girls to dance?" Perry still couldn't quite believe it. He'd never heard of a teacher doing anything at the noon dance except scowl at students and act bored.

"Absolutely, and the girls are eating it up. Take a gander yourself. He just got through slow dancing with the French exchange dish, and now he is out there with Amber."

Sure enough there was the handsome coach twirling Amber around the floor while the record player blasted out *Only You* by The Platters.

"How long has this been going on?" asked Perry.

"All week," replied Johnson. "Every day the crowd gets bigger."

"Oh, oh," mumbled Williams. "Look out. Here comes the Gestapo."

Entering the room were a stern-faced Mr. Beasely and a heavyset woman carrying a huge handbag. They appeared to be on a mission.

"Who's the lard bucket?" hissed Williams.

"It's old lady Fitzmorris," answered Johnson. "She's the PTA president and always sticking her big behind into school stuff."

Perry thought hard. It must be Janice Fitzmorris' mother. Janice was a certified math brain and the darling of Mrs. Burkett's trigonometry class. She seemed nice enough, but he'd heard her mother was something else. There was some story floating around about how Mr. Fitzmorris had suddenly walked out of the house a few months ago, and shortly thereafter had been arrested in Reno for shooting holes in a blackjack table with his World War II .45 caliber pistol. True or false, Mr. Fitzmorris had not been seen around New Rose for some months.

Beasely and Mrs. Fitzmorris pushed through the ring of onlookers and stood on the edge of the dance floor. Beasely visibly winced when the music started again; this time *Mr. Sandman* by the Chordettes. Mrs. Fitzmorris pulled a clipboard from her voluminous purse and began scribbling.

"Oh boy, oh boy," whispered Johnson. "I'm sure they're checking out the the coach."

"Yeah," agreed Williams, "Mr. Mac is up guano creek for sure."

The buzzer sounded ending the lunch period, and students, after issuing their customary loud groans, began ambling off to 4th period classes. Perry noticed that Beasely had grabbed Coach McIntyre by the elbow and was talking to him in an agitated manner. Mrs. Fitzmorris waddled out into the hallway.

Johnson poked Perry between the ribs. "So, whaddya think? Will Beasely give Coach 30 lashes with a wet noodle?"

Williams snickered. "Or maybe have him stay after school and run some laps in the rain?'"

"I dunno," answered Perry. "But I'll bet you a dollar to a doughnut that whatever Beasely does won't hold a candle to what old lady Fitzmorris might cook up."

Chapter Nine
The Game

October, with its granite skies and pelting rain, found the New Rose football team floundering. After barely winning an opening game against Vernonia, a clumsy non-league foe, the Thorns had lost three straight and now faced the dismal prospect of playing the Central Catholic Saints—big, mean and ranked fifth in the state.

Rival coaches described the Thorns as "intelligent" and "spunky." Translated, this meant they were undersized and a bit soft. Only Vernon Grover scaled more than 200 pounds. Archie Mickleson, the starting quarterback, was five feet four inches tall. True, Williams was a gifted running back, but he couldn't count on much help from his scrawny linemen. Central Catholic would probably outweigh the Thorns by 20 to 30 pounds per player; a fact looming large in the minds of those slated to start.

In practices the week prior to the game the team's attitude was distinctly morose. Despite Coach Gunderson's pep talks, the players tended to act like inmates on death row. No matter what the coaches cooked up, they knew this was going to hurt. Last minute stays of execution—like having the game canceled by measles epidemics or Martian invasions were popular fantasies.

Naturally, new coach McIntyre viewed the upcoming clash differently. He preferred to call it a "terrific challenge, a game to test what we're made of. After all," he boomed, "it's not the size of the body; it's the size of the heart." Behind him, head coach Gunderson nodded and folded his arms.

"Geez," whispered Perry. "Go tell that to Al Sobrinski." Sobrinski was Central Catholic's 230 pound defensive tackle whose legs were so muscle-bound he didn't wear thigh pads. He had been thrown out for unnecessary roughness in last week's game against the Beaverton Beavers. "He must have a 230 pound heart."

McIntyre warmed to his subject, ignoring Perry's muttered responses.

"They put on their pants just like you guys, one foot at a time!"

"Yeah, but what goes in those pants is huge!"

"Believe in yourselves. Think positive!"

"We believe we're going to get our butts kicked."

"Miracles do happen."

"But those guys are Catholic. They've got all those saints on their side."

Once the dreaded Friday night arrived, several of the Thorns hid out on the long hall leading to the visitor's locker room. When CC trooped in wearing street clothes, Marty Bickerstaff, the Thorn's feisty 145-pound split end, sneered, "Hey, they don't look all that big." But to Perry, they looked plenty big enough. And plenty cocky, too, brimming with the confidence that comes with stomping other teams with monotonous regularity.

As it turned out, the Thorns made a game of it. Not because of undaunted courage, however. Several unpredictable factors intervened. For starters, the weather, while not quite up to hurricane standards, was chillingly wet and windy. A classic Oregon monsoon descended on the field right after the opening Kickoff, and Central's high-scoring passing attack went in the toilet. The ball quickly became "slicker than cat spit," to use Williams' expression, and Central's all state quarterback, Vince Mullenhoffer, fumbled twice on scoring drives.

New Rose's dog-eared football field contributed to the erratic play. The JV's had played on it in the afternoon and had chewed up the already splotchy grass turf. By half time it was a quagmire, with the two teams rooting in the mud like prize porkers at the neighboring truck farms. Even big Al Sobrinski had trouble with his footing. Oliver Hill upended him once by sliding under Al's feet in the manner of Willie Mays stealing second base.

Just before the half, Perry, making a rare appearance on the defensive line, scrambled in pursuit of Central's quarterback. He fell over a blocker and stood up just in time to be hit squarely in the chest with an errant pass. In four years of high school, Perry had never caught or carried a football. He stood stunned for a second while the ball clung to his mud-caked jersey. Then he wrapped both arms around the elusive pigskin and began plodding upfield, running as though snarling Rotweilers were at his heels. Tackled somewhere around midfield, he careened wildly into the visitor's bench, knocking flat Central's rotund principal who always accompanied the team. "Give my regards to the Pope," Perry gloated as he stumbled back on the field.

Johnson, sent in briefly while Williams shook off a charley horse, became so excited he attempted to throw a vicious—for him—cross body block on Zack Murphy, Central's six-foot-six linebacker. "OOP," mumbled Murphy as he shook Johnson off like some pesky insect. "Owww," grimaced Johnson as he slid down Murphy's muddy leg and grabbed the linebacker's shoelaces. Murphy toppled like a giant sequoia, while his assailant hastily rolled out of the way. "What kind of chickencrap are you trying to pull?" screamed Murphy.

"The chickens are coming home to roost, that's what!" replied Johnson as we wiped mud from his helmet.

Late in the fourth quarter, the Thorns began to breathe a bit easier. "We may get out of this alive," grinned Williams who had actually managed to catch a pass and hang on to it, one of only two completed by New Rose that night.

With three minutes to go, Coach Gunderson sent in the play of the year, the one old Thorns would talk about for years to come. Mickleson, the pint-sized quarterback, took the ball from underneath the center, faked a handoff, and seemed to run a bootleg around the right end. In the blur of mud, rain and colliding bodies, Mickleson had actually placed the ball on the ground behind the bent leg of his diminutive right guard, Vigil "Pee" Martin, who had lined up next to the center. Martin deliberately flubbed his blocking assignment and the Central defenders surged through, chasing Mickleson en masse and gang tackling the runt with glee. Martin then scooped up the ball, shielded it with his body, turned and chugged 50 yards through the muck to score. The 30 or so hearty fans remaining, huddled under umbrellas, went crazy, and Central's coach slammed his clipboard to the ground in anguish.

"Hey," grinned Kingfisher as the rain-soaked Thorns ran to the locker room after the final gun, "it's sort of a moral victory, losing only 33-7 to those guys."

"Yeah," agreed Williams. "Did you notice how happy coach McIntyre was hugging all those rally girls? Even that Frenchie Francoise came over and gave him a smooch."

"Okay, Okay!" hooted Perry. "Now bring on those hicks from Scappoose. We'll cream 'em."

November, 1954 News Flashes

The Teamsters Union ends a yearlong strike against Pittsburgh department stores after winning a 5-cent hourly wage increase with a promise of further increases next year.

Kenya, Africa, security forces launch a drive against Mau Mau terrorists operating 40 miles from Nairobi.

UCLA, Ohio State and Oklahoma State are named the nation's top college football teams in a poll of coaches.

The first Godzilla film is released in Japan.

In Sylacauga, Alabama, a 4-kilogram sulfide meteorite crashes through a roof, bounces off a radio and hits a woman, giving her a bad bruise. This is the first known modern case of a space rock hitting a human.

★ NEW ROSE BUD ★

The Student Newspaper of New Rose High School

Volume XI, Number 3   *Friday, November 12, 1954*

New Home Ec Book Gives Tips to Gals

According to Home Economics teacher Miss Lepage, the class's new text book offers girls some valuable advice on "How to be a good wife." Tips Include:

Have dinner ready. Most men are hungry when they come home from work, and the prospect of a good meal is part of the needed warm welcome.

Prepare yourself. Be a little gay and a little more interesting. His boring day may need a lift.

Minimize all noise. Eliminate all noise of the washer, dryer or vacuum. Encourage the children to be quiet. Greet him with a smile.

Make the evening his. Never complain if he does not take you out to dinner or places of entertainment.

Some don'ts: Don't greet him with problems or complaints. Don't complain if he is late for dinner. Make him comfortable. Arrange his pillow and offer to take off his shoes.

Miss Lepage did say that she had heard about the textbook's author recently filing for divorce.

Boys Pass NROTC Exams

(Story on page two, inside)

Chapter Ten
Whispers Start

With the end of football season, and another three-win, five-loss record, Perry found himself at loose ends after school. He tried out for the basketball team, but being short, slow and nearsighted, was quickly cut. Johnson suffered the same fate and was talking about working again at the local Dairy Queen. Williams, Sherwood and Kingfisher did make the varsity squad, and Perry was thinking about asking to keep stats so he could hang around the gym and keep track of the guys he knew. He briefly considered going out for wrestling because Mr. McIntyre had been named assistant coach, but decided, no. It just didn't have the sex appeal of basketball.

He was sitting in the pullout bleachers waiting for practice to start, when Lance Bishop came over and plopped down beside him. Lance had only been at New Rose for one year and was considered something of a mystery. He had played on the Thorn's football team with Perry, but they rarely spoke to each other. He favored tight, white T-shirts, wore his hair long and combed it back ducktail fashion. Perry wasn't sure what to make of him, but admired his "I don't-care-what-you-think-about-me" attitude. Girls said Lance reminded them of James Dean, and were delighted to discover he was silky-smooth on the noon dance floor.

"Hey," said Lance. "Think these spastics will win anything this year?"

"That's the $64 question," answered Perry.

"The guys will have their hands full, coping with McCready," Lance said, pulling a comb from his jacket pocket. Skeeter McCready was the varsity basketball coach and a man known for his short-fuse temper. There were still dents in the dressing room wall where he had thrown a folding chair after a loss last year.

"Yeah, well, it's either deal with McCready or forget about playing."

Lance shrugged. "As far as I'm concerned, the only coach around here worth a damn is McIntyre, and I think old Beasely is out to get him."

Perry scratched his nose. "What makes you say that?"

"I was up in the office yesterday, and by chance I overheard the school secretary talking on the phone to a friend. She was saying she's repeatedly heard Beasely yakking on the phone with somebody about how teachers shouldn't be seen dancing with students."

Perry remembered the noon dance confrontation between the coach and Beasely. But that had been weeks ago, and he had heard McIntyre no longer made that scene. "I thought that noon dance stuff was all dead and buried."

"Not as far as Beasely is concerned. It seems this same woman phones almost every day, and according to the secretary, Beasely always gets red in the face when he takes the call. It's got to be about McIntyre. Plus, now there's a rumor going around that McIntyre was seen Saturday night with one of the cheerleaders."

The gym floor was now filled with varsity and JV players dribbling basketballs and firing up shots at the backboards on the sides as well as the ends of the court. The din they created made it hard to hear what Lance was saying. A ball crashed into the stands in front of them, and Perry bent down to hurl it back on the floor.

"That sounds crazy, Lance. Teachers don't date students. It'd be a breach of contract or some such thing."

"Don't be so sure. Just remember who's the yell queen. It's Amber Kelly, and she looks a lot older than seventeen."

Perry considered the possibility. Amber had a reputation of being a hot number, and she was always wearing those really tight pedal pushers. But, surely McIntyre wouldn't be so stupid. Or, would he? "It's just rumors anyway, isn't it? Nobody's got any proof, do they?"

Lance got up to leave. "Yeah, but you know what they say: 'where there's smoke, there's fire,' and this place is ripe for some juicy gossip. In fact now there's a story floating around claiming Beasely is up to some hanky-panky."

"No kidding? What's the story?"

Lance shook his head. "I gotta go. But if you want the scoop, find The Mouse. He claims he's got the inside stuff. And I'll give you a big hint: it involves our oo-la-la exchange student."

Perry still couldn't believe what Lance claimed, but he resolved to look up The Mouse the first chance he got. "Wouldn't it be great if Beasely got caught messing around," he thought as he left the gym.

Chapter Eleven
The Mouse Talks

It took Perry a few minutes to zero in on where Eddie "The Mouse" was sitting in the cafeteria. He wasn't at his usual spot next to Monty Carpenter, and Perry had heard some rumor that Monty was thinking about dropping out and joining the Army, or maybe it was the Navy. Perry couldn't remember which.

This day The Mouse was way over on the far side of the cavernous room, sitting by himself and shoveling in macaroni and cheese from his tray. Perry ambled over with his sack lunch and sat across from him.

"Slumming?" asked The Mouse.

"Yeah. I thought it would be cool to sit next to a real jerkoff for a change," answered Perry.

"Where are your hot dog buddies today? Off sucking up to the powers that be?" The Mouse gulped down a spoonful of cherry red Jell-O.

"Were in a hurry to get down to the noon dance I guess." Perry said, pulling the wax paper from his sandwich. "I wasn't interested."

The Mouse wiped his mouth with a wrinkled handkerchief. "So, why are you suddenly returning to this table, pray tell? I have a feeling you're not here to inquire about my health."

"Actually, I was wondering how you were getting along in the parley voo class. Tell me true, Mouse, is our Frenchie exchange student worth it?"

The Mouse grinned, flashing his yellow teeth. "You know, Perry, no dame is worth it, but it has been fun seeing her in action. If she wears sweaters any tighter, she'll split the yarn open. And it's not just us yahoo students who are noticing."

"You mean Coach McIntyre?"

The Mouse chuckled. "McIntryre, Smackintyre. He sniffs all the good-looking girls, but he's got a big strike against him when it comes to Francoise. He doesn't speak French. In fact, outside of Miss Ringwater I believe there is only one other adult in this dump who speaks the lingo, and he occupies a large office up front."

Perry considered that fact. He remembered what Lance Bishop had hinted about. Was The Mouse suggesting that their principal was getting cozy with Francoise? It seemed bizarre. Mr. Beasely was at least 30 years older, maybe more, and you could hardly call him charming. Still there had been a story in the *Bud* last year about him attending some French-American educational conference. Or was it Spanish-American?

"Come on, Mouse. Be real. You can't mean Beasely, can you?"

The Mouse leaned across the table. "Maybe I can, maybe I can't. Right now only the *Shadow* knows, and he ain't talking. But chew on this, Perry, old boy: Yours truly has been working nights for the past month as a bus boy at the Timber Topper."

Perry squinted. The Timber Topper was a local night spot east of New Rose, out on the Clackamas River. Perry had never been inside the place but he had heard it was so dark inside the waitresses used little flashlights to write their orders.

"So?"

"So, I get a good look at the customers who ask for the booths in the darkest corners—corners as dark as say, *the Bastille*." He looked enormously pleased with himself. "And consider this, Perry: guess what club I've joined this year?"

Perry blinked. Club? The Mouse was a noted social-outcast and loner. What club would want him?

"Can't guess, can you? Well, Daddy-O, you are looking at the next Cecil B. DeMille. I've joined the New Rose Camera Club, and among other goodies, you get to borrow their brand new Bell & Howell

Super 8mm home movie camera. Now, Perry, in your puny little brain do you happen to know what's next door to the Timber Topper?"

It took Perry a couple of minutes to reply. "Some kind of motel?"

"Exactly," said The Mouse. "None other than the Sweet Dreams Motel, and I'm sure you've heard of its reputation?"

"Isn't it kind of sleazy?

The Mouse chuckled. "Let's just say that it will never be confused with the Waldorf-Astoria. But the most interesting thing about the Sweet Dreams is that my uncle's the night manager."

"And?" Perry looked perplexed.

"And, he knows some tricks about certain rooms. Tricks that might interest a person like me who wants to make motion picture history. Yes, Perry, one of these days *movies are going to be better than ever*. And, maybe, just maybe, you smartasses are going to remember The Mouse for more than just my bad teeth." He grabbed his tray and stood up. "See you later, alligator," he said and smugly sauntered away, leaving Perry staring forlornly at the table.

Was Lance right? Did The Mouse really have the goods on old Man Beasely? Or was he just blowing smoke in the hope of finally getting noticed? The blaring of the buzzer interrupted Perry's thoughts. If he didn't hurry, he'd be late for Senior English. He broke into a dogtrot and headed for his locker. "What next?' he wondered. One way or another, either McIntyre or Beasely were sure to keep things interesting in the weeks ahead.

December, 1954 News Flashes

Dr. Jonas Salk reports that Infantile Paralysis (Polio) will be eradicated when susceptible age groups are effectively vaccinated, according to results of tests of the Salk Anti-Polio Vaccine.

Auto gas prices rise to 29 cents a gallon.

The US Senate votes 67 to 22 to condemn Senator Joseph McCarthy for "conduct that tends to bring the Senate into dishonor and disrepute."

An Associated Press poll of sportswriters and broadcasters selects NY Giants center fielder Willie Mays as all-sport "Athlete of the Year."

★ NEW ROSE BUD ★

The Student Newspaper of New Rose High School

Volume XI, Number 4   *Friday, December 17, 1954*

Bachelor Living Class Prepares Succulent Sea Foods

Aromas reminiscent of "Davey Jones Locker" floated through the halls last Friday as the Bachelor Living Class prepared sea food luncheons.

"The boys did a swell job of cooking the cuisine of fish and chips," said their teacher, Miss Lepage.

The class is learning much in the art of Home Economics and is being instructed about some of the social graces of eating. The week before saw the "chefs-to-be" cooked spaghetti and accomplished the feat of twirling it smartly on a fork.

"Best of all, we haven't poisoned anybody yet," said senior Oliver Hill.

Curfew Act Curbs Hours

Oregon's curfew law has returned to its winter schedule. Deadlines for those 14 or older is 10:15 PM on school nights, and 12:00 midnight on Friday and Saturday nights.

"New Rose students who violate the curfew will find themselves in extremely hot water," said Principal B. Beasely.

Chapter Twelve
A Close Encounter

It was fifth period and almost all of the members of the New Rose student body had trooped reluctantly into the auditorium for a special assembly arranged by Principal Beasley. Each year for reasons that escaped both faculty and students, Mr. Beasley brought in a fraternity brother named Dr. Richard Risley Mountebank to show slides of his travels through Canada, Mexico, Cuba, the Florida Keys and Central America.

Dr. Mountebank, a lanky, sour-faced man with thinning hair and a pencil mustache, was seriously lacking in charisma. Perry remembered all too well last year's assembly when the good doctor's droning monotone put Vernon Grover so solidly asleep that his snores had to be muzzled with Becky Winslow's wool scarf. When the slide projector jammed with five minutes to go, the audience erupted in spontaneous applause and marched out before principal Beasely could restore order.

This year, unknown to his classmates, Perry had managed to convince his home room teacher, Mr. Brimmer, that he desperately needed to be excused from the assembly so he could spend the hour in the library doing research for his senior English paper. Mr. Brimmer was not thrilled with his decision, however, and made Perry swear not to mention it to anyone. "Otherwise, I'll have your whole gang trying to sneak into the library!"

So, when the buzzer blared to announce 5th period, Perry hung back as the others headed for the auditorium. He ducked into the boy's lavatory and stood in one of the stalls until he heard the hall noise die down. Then, he stealthily hustled down the hall and turned quickly into the library, where Miss Gimbell greeted him with folded arms and a look that would curdle milk. She was a skinny, pale woman of indeterminate age who was fond of dresses with puffy sleeves. Woe to any student who messed up her tidy shelves.

"I'm legal, Miss Gimbell," said Perry offering her the hall pass signed by Mr. Brimmer. "It's really important that I look up stuff on William Randolph Hearst for Senior English."

"Hummmf," replied Miss Gimbell. "Well, there is a shelf of biographies of famous men in the back of the room. Why don't you help yourself, while I look in on the assembly? Personally, I've always enjoyed Dr. Mountebank's presentations."

Perry went directly behind the ceiling-high metal shelves in the rear of the room, thankful that Miss Gimbell wouldn't be breathing down his neck. As soon as he squeezed between the shelves, he discovered he wasn't alone in the library. In fact, he nearly fell over the crouched figure who had been kneeling while she placed books on the lower shelf.

"*Bon jour,*" the figure said with a giggle. "You should watch where you are stepping, *n'est ce pas?*"

"Geez, I'm sorry," gasped Perry, wondering what he should say next. "I didn't see you."

She stood up cradling several thick books. "Well, I deedn't see you either so, *touche*', we are even, no? *Tres bien.* I'm Francoise and who are you?"

"Uh, Perry. Perry Palmer."

"Eees nice to meet you. *Comment allez-vous?*" She stuck out her hand and Perry, after momentarily wondering if he should kiss it, gave her a weak handshake. He noticed she was wearing one of her trademark extra snug sweaters, this one with a frilly collar. "I've seen you before from a deestance, Perry. I thought you looked like someone I knew in Paree. Are your parents French? Do you *parlez vous Francais?*" She tossed a wisp of hair aside and smiled warmly.

Perry thrust his hands deep into the pocket of his cords. "No, or at least I don't think so, and I can barely speak English, let alone anything French." He made an effort to take his eyes off her sweater and was startled to see how full and red her lips were. He noted that her eyes were a stunning shade of green.

"*Sacre bleu*, but you look French to me. You have a certain *savoir-faire*. Are you sure you don't have some ancestors who were *combattants* with Napoleon?" She smoothly slipped two books onto the shelf by Perry's shoulder.

Perry swallowed hard. "Um, well, I have this uncle who claims there was a Palmer who sailed with Jean Lafitte."

"Jean Lafitte, *mon dieu!*" She shook her head in mock dismay. "Wasn't he a *pirate?*"

"Yeah, but at least he was French!" Perry was delighted to see that she laughed at his reply. Why was it, he wondered, that it was so blasted difficult to figure out what to say to cute girls.

"Now, if you'll *excusez-moi*, Mr. Perry the pirate, I have to slip by you and go *tout de suite* to the office. Mr. Beasely wanted me to come by after library duty to meet zees Doctor something or other." She brushed past Perry, just touching him enough to make him tingle. "*Au revoir*," she said, heading for the door.

"Yeah, well, happy parlay voo or whatever." Perry winced. Probably that was a dumb thing to say.

Francoise looked back over her shoulder. "Too bad you're not in French class, *mon ami*. I could help you apply the *coupe de grace* to your homework." She stopped at the door. "Why don't you call me sometime? We could discuss Monsieur LaFitte and the rest of your *extraordinaire* ancestors."

Perry spent the rest of the period staring at the first page of "The Life of William Randoph Hearst" and wondering what to make of his chance encounter with the curvy French exchange student. She seemed awfully friendly, didn't she? Not stuck up at all. Didn't seem to be anything like those smug rally squad girls like Amy and Sandy. Did she really mean it when she said, "call me?" What would I say if I did call? "Hi, I'm the doofus who fell on you in the library?"

His musings were interrupted by the return of Miss Gimball. "You missed a very stimulating presentation, Perry. Dr. Mountebank showed some slides of the Everglades that were remarkable—a little dark, perhaps, but still remarkable. Did you find the book you needed?"

Perry nodded and closed the cover on William Randolph Hearst. "Um, yes, I did, but now, Miss Gimball, I do have another question."

"And that is?"

"Does the library have any books about Jean Lafitte?"

After dinner that night Perry went into the breakfast nook to phone Kingfisher. Perry never could understand why his mother wanted their one telephone located in such a distant portion of the house. He further wondered why she insisted on keeping the coal black wall model. To Perry it looked like the phone you would find on the walls of cheap restaurants.

Perry reasoned that Kingfisher was the guy who seemed to have the most success with girls. Maybe he could offer some tips on how to deal with Francoise. As luck would have it, Kingfisher answered on the first ring and was happy to have Perry drop by.

Sitting in Kingfisher's living room Perry was aware he sounded a bit like a sixth grader who had just received a valentine from the cute girl next door. "What do you think? Should I call her? Do you think she'd go out with me? What do you hear about her?"

"Perry, my lad, you have been snockered, but let me quickly add, you are far from the first to be so smitten. This Francoise babe rolls her eyes at everything in pants, but just try to follow up and whammo, you receive the deep freeze treatment." Kingfisher paused to cough loudly into a handkerchief. He and Johnson had been fighting colds for more than a week, and when Perry had casually mentioned it to his mother, she had replied, "That's what happens when you refuse to wear a hat. I wouldn't be surprised to hear they're in bed with double pneumonia."

"But, geez, she really seemed kind of interested in me."

"Oh, sure, and someday jackrabbits will fly to the moon. Come on, Perry, face facts. This dame is only interested in older types. She's been dating some college guy and, you know all about the Beasely rumors." Kingfisher blew his nose loudly into his now yellow-stained handkerchief.

"Yeah, yeah, rumors, schumors. Nobody's got any proof."

"Maybe not yet, but trust old Dr. Kingfisher, something's going on. I can smell it."

Perry leaned back and sighed. "So, what should I do?"

Kingfisher coughed hard and pointed to the telephone on the table in the hallway. "Simple. Pick up Alexander Graham Bell's invention and give Frenchy a call. And get ready for me to shout, 'I told you so.'"

Perry hesitated. "Well, I did look up her phone number before I came over here."

"Now or never," sniffed Kingfisher from behind his handkerchief.

Perry picked up the phone and dialed AL 3-9485. An older, male voice answered. Perry guessed it must be Mr. DuPrey. "Hello, sir. Could I speak to Francoise, please?"

"Sure. Why not? She loves calls from boys." Mr. DuPrey sounded tired. "What's your name?"

"It's Perry. Perry Palmer."

Mr. DuPrey clanked down the receiver and Perry could hear him call out, "Franny. It's for you. Another boy. I think he said his name was Larry."

"Allo. Eezz zis Larry?"

"No, Francoise, this is Perry."

"*Qui*, Who?"

"Perry Palmer. I fell on top of you today in the library."

"You deed?"

"Yeah, and you said maybe give you a call."

"I deed?"

"Un-huh. Maybe talk about Jean Lafitte."

"Zeen Labeet? *Alors*, I gees I don't reemember. It was such a beezy day."

"Oh."

"Leesten, *excusez-moi* but I thought you were Larry. And would you mind hanging up *s'il vous plait*? I'm so sorry but I know Larry is trying to *telephone* me long deestance. You understand, no?"

"I guess so."

"*C'magnifique.* Thank you so much, Barry. *Merci beau coup.*"

The line went dead.

Perry resisted the urge to throw the receiver at the grinning Kingfisher. "She thought I was some guy named Barry."

"Figures. You're lucky she talked to you at all. Now you know firsthand what it's like to receive the Royal Shaft."

Perry pulled his jacket back on. "Well, thanks for nothing. I hope you cough yourself into a zombie."

"My pleasure. Dr. Kingfisher's advice to the lonely hearts is always available to good, if a bit stupid, friends."

Perry headed for the door. "Maybe I'll start a new chapter of the Hermits."

Kingfisher stifled a sneeze. "Better yet, start a club for the 'Frozen by Francoise.' You won't be hurting for members."

Chapter Thirteen
Christmas Break

Christmas break at New Rose H.S. was not an especially happy time for Perry. He had no brothers or sisters, and except for his gruff Uncle Bob, there were no close relatives. His mother tried to inject some holiday spirit into their small home, insisting that Perry bring home a traditional tree and help her decorate it with an overcoat of silvery foil ice cycles. However, once this was accomplished, she reverted back to her prevailing moods of worry and fear. Any fleeting notion of Yuletide joy quickly evaporated.

She was older than the mothers of Perry's friends and Perry felt she was hopelessly out of touch with the times. He wished she would dress in something besides shapeless drab dresses that accentuated her short, dumpy figure. He regretted that she had few interests in life other than himself and the Christian Science Church. Her strongest beliefs centered around the words of Mary Baker Eddy and the merits of living frugally. The idea of spending much for Christmas gifts was as a foreign to her as eating in a fancy restaurant. Perry knew better than to expect much under the tree.

Since his dad had died when he was eleven, the custom at the Palmer house was for Perry and his mother to open packages on Christmas eve, and then on the following afternoon drive to Uncle Bob's for a boring ham dinner.

The gift exchange in recent years had become painful for Perry because his mother continually misread all his hints and produced unappealing presents. To his dismay, she insisted on annually giving him a new pair of flannel pajamas, which had been carefully selected from the Montgomery Ward holiday catalog. Last year she had compounded his disappointment by presenting him with her special version of a trendy cap favored by all his friends. Off the shelf it was simply a lightweight poplin hat in various colors complete with a turn-down brim. However, to Perry's mom, it seemed far too wimpy to wear in the rain-swept winter months. "I don't understand why you can't wear your wool stocking cap and be happy," she had complained. She felt she had solved the issue by sewing in a lining made from some of Perry's old wool socks. "This should keep you from catching a horrible cold," she proclaimed as he unwrapped the package.

When school resumed Perry had attempted to wear the cap as though it were identical to those of his buddies. His efforts at concealing the lining were successful for awhile, but he had forgotten how fiercely the east wind could blow in January. Racing through the New Rose parking lot, an unexpected gust blew off the cap in front of Williams and Johnson, and Perry knew he couldn't live it down.

"What is this?" crowed Johnson, picking up the offending cap and tossing it to a wide-eyed Williams. "Some new fashion, no doubt favored by Alaskan Eskimos?"

"Perry, this is too much," said Williams, holding the cap just out of reach of the distraught Perry. "And what a lovely argyle pattern. Were these last worn when you had that case of athlete's foot?"

Afterward Perry would wear the cap when leaving home and then stick it under the front seat of the Chevy as he neared the school. Still, Williams and Johnson wasted little time in spreading the word that in all of New Rose only Perry Palmer could be found wearing a hat lined with wool socks. Once again Amy Quinton and Sandy Smith found great amusement in Perry's embarrassment.

"Did you wear your wooly head sox today, Perry?" they would call, as he wrestled books from his locker.

This year, Perry was silently praying for a change of fortune. He had mentioned repeatedly that the jacket of choice for seniors at New

Rose was a leather aviator's model—the kind worn by aces in World War II. Yes, it was expensive for their budget, but after all it was his senior year, and he hadn't asked for anything special in a long time. "Besides," he had explained to his mother, "I probably would never catch a cold wearing this kind of jacket." "And maybe for once I wouldn't feel so dang chilly in this house," he thought. As usual he wasn't sure, but he thought his message was sinking in. To enhance his chances, he made sure she knew he was going to give her those fuzzy red slippers she had admired in the Wards catalog.

So, Christmas eve, 1954, found Perry and his mother sitting in their compact living room directly in front of their icicle-draped Douglas fir. She sank back in the one darkly upholstered easy chair she favored while Perry fidgeted nervously on the edge of the matching davenport. Yellowish light from a large ceiling fixture flooded the room's center, while somber shadows dominated the corners. Perry, unable to wait any longer, suddenly lunged forward and grabbed from beneath the tree a large package covered in cheap red Christmas wrapping paper.

"Well!" gasped his mother. "I guess you're ready to open your presents."

"I guess I am," said Perry. "It's time, isn't it?"

"I'm sure Santa Claus wouldn't mind," said his mother, carefully folding her hands over her lap.

Perry ripped the paper savagely, thinking to himself, "It's a box big enough to hold a jacket. Am I finally getting what I wanted?" He slowly pulled back the lid of the cardboard box and caught the unmistakable whiff of leather. "Oh boy," he thought, and yanked off the lid of the carton. "Oh, no," he sighed under his breath.

It was indeed a leather jacket and in the proper dark cordovan color. It looked to be the right size. But there was one glaring problem: It had a fuzzy, fur-lined collar. None of his friend's jackets had collars that looked like this. Theirs all were smooth and easily turned up. Theirs looked like those worn by Jimmy Stewart and Clark Gable in the war movies. This one looked like something a North Dakota farmer might wear.

His mother was smiling. "I think this style is so much better than those with plain collars, don't you agree, Perry? So much warmer, I'm sure."

"Well, thanks, mom," said Perry with eyes downcast.

"Oh, don't mention it," said his mother. "I just knew it would be the right thing."

"Sure," said Perry, fingering the furry material. "I wonder," he thought, "could I shave this off, or maybe peel it some way, like skinning a rabbit?"

His mother pointed under the tree. "Merry Christmas, Perry, and don't forget to open that other package. I have a feeling it just might be something to keep you warm when you go to bed tonight."

January, 1955 News Flashes

Atomic Energy Commission Chairman Lewis Strauss reports that the US nuclear arms stockpile "is growing rapidly."

RCA demonstrates first music synthesizer.

TV and newsreel cameras film a presidential press conference for the first time, releasing parts of it for broadcast and theater showing.

Congress passes bill authorizing mobilization of US troops should China attack Taiwan.

Georgia Tech's basketball team defeats Kentucky, 59-58, Kentucky's first loss in 130 home games.

Actor Kevin Costner is born.

★ NEW ROSE BUD ★

The Student Newspaper of New Rose High School

Volume XI, Number 5   *January 13, 1955*

Ypres Winter Formal Planned for Next Sat

"Blue violins will be the theme of this year's winter formal which is going to be held in Arthur Murray's main ballroom downtown.,

Saturday, Jan. 21, from 7:00 to 11:00 PM. "It's the first time Arthur Murray's has ever rented one of their ballrooms to a school club," said Ypres Club Prexy Amber Kelly. "It's going to be fabulous." Pam Tucker was named decorations chairman.

Photographer Wanted To Take Pics for the Bud

WANTED!! One photographer complete with flash bulbs to take pictures for the BUD.

When Sparky Kirkpatrick left school to join the Marines, the BUD lost its only picture taker and now we are in a dilly of a pickle. Contact the advisor, Mr. Willits.

PEP Problems Continue

"Pep assemblies have been dropping in attendance until lately it doesn't seem worth even having them," said SB President Raymond Kingfisher at a recent Student Council meeting.

Several suggestions were made to improve attendance including starting a jazz band and having a dunk tank for coaches.

Chapter Fourteen
Rocky Butte

For reasons Perry found amusing, the New Rose H.S. faculty decreed that all Friday night after-basketball-game dances had to end at 11:00 PM. That way, hoped the adults, all students would go more or less right home and be off the streets at least by midnight.

Fat chance. After the last 45 record was yanked off the turntable, and Fats Domino crooned *Ain't It a Shame* for the final dance, it still seemed way too early to say good night. The noisy throng spilled out of the gym and into the shadowy parking lot, adrenaline and hormones flowing, ready for any kind of action that the evening might offer.

On a regular basis, however, the evening's offerings were not exactly rip-roaring. Guys with cars who had dates tore off for dark lanes hoping to improve their knowledge of female anatomy. Guys like Perry, without dates, hung around the parking lot trying to figure out what to do, which frequently was not much of anything.

A stop at Jim Dandy's Drive-In was always an option—obligatory for those with dates—but it called for the spending of money which was constantly in short supply. Plus, it was demoralizing for those without girlfriends to have to gaze upon those lucky louts who did, and who delighted in flaunting their good fortune.

At the back of the graveled parking area, Perry found Johnson who was equally at loose ends, and the two spent a few minutes bemoaning the results of the basketball game played prior to the dance. The Astoria Fighting Fishermen had shellacked the Thorns because they couldn't stop a thick-necked, broad-shouldered center from muscling his way to the basket. "Sherwood and Williams must be off somewhere licking their wounds by now," said Johnson.

"Yeah, and Kingfisher too, I guess," replied Perry.

"In a pig's eye," boomed a voice from behind them. "I just saw them headed for a party at Amber's house." Perry turned and saw it was Vernon Grover, the chubby tackle on the football team. "But don't despair that you didn't get invited," continued Grover, "because I have a grand plan for tonight, and I need you two to help me pull it off."

Grover's main claim to fame was his one-of-a-kind automobile, a genuine 1939 Willys Overland Sedan. Perry could barely see the machine parked nearby, close to the fence. Snub-nosed and powered by a four-cylinder, 63 hp engine, it easily started with a push when the battery conked out, which happened routinely.

Grinning gleefully, Grover urged the duo to come over and look in the Willy's cramped back seat. There was no dome light, and at first it was impossible to see anything in the murky shadows, but gradually Perry could make out the shape of some kind of metal cylinder with a skinny hose attached near the bottom.

"It's my uncle's hand pump sprayer," proclaimed Grover. "He uses it for his apple trees. Just look at this little beauty! It'll hold a full three gallons, and pumped up, it'll shoot out a stream that'll blow away a bumblebee at twenty feet."

"So?" snarled Johnson. "What's that mean for us? You want to raid some apple farm?"

"No, you dumbbell! Armed with this weapon we can now motor up to Rocky Butte and terrorize those dorks who are parked there in cars making out."

Rocky Butte, a turret-shaped mound of basalt on the edge of town, was noteworthy for two reasons: the antiquated county jail was situated on one side, and at the top there were plenty of secluded parking spots with great night views of twinkling city lights. The latter provided a time-honored excuse for lovers to pull over and engage in various amorous maneuvers.

"Wait a minute," demanded Perry. "What's the point of spraying a bunch of parked cars with steamed up windows?"

Grover snickered. "Don't you get it, Pearshape? We're going to get 'em to roll down those steamy windows. That's why I need you two to make it work. First, I drive up right beside some passion pit car and shine my spotlight inside. Then, Perry, you're in the front passenger seat, and you roll down your window and shout something about an emergency, or it's a matter of life and death, or whatever will get the poor sucker to roll down his window to check what's going on."

"And that's when we douse 'em," interrupted Johnson.

"Precisely! Or more to the point, you douse 'em, 'cause you've been lying down in the back seat with the window wide open and little Betsy, here, all pumped up. When the yahoo's window goes down, you pop up and let him have it."

"It just might work," muttered Johnson.

"Hold on," Perry objected. "What if this guy's got a baseball bat or a gun and comes after us? Whadda we do then?"

Grover shrugged. "We just got to move really fast. Our lights are out and we leave the motor running. By the time our pigeon wipes the water out of his eyes, we'll have beat a hasty retreat and he won't be able to catch us."

"It just might work," repeated Johnson.

"Plus, here's our ace in the hole," added Grover. "I added a batch of red food coloring to the water. That way when the guy wipes it off his face, it'll look like blood. He'll think he's been hit with some lethal ray gun and he's bleeding like a stuck pig. He'll be in such a panic, we'll get away easy."

"It's worth a try," said Johnson, as all three piled into the Willys which, amazingly, started without needing to be pushed.

Soon they were on the moonlit crest of Rocky Butte where the trio selected their first victim with great care, using all the predatory skills of adolescent Bengal tigers. It was a banged-up, older Ford sedan parked suspiciously at an odd angle to the road. The chrome-laden front bumper nestled between boulders the size of giant beach balls. It would take some wheel-tugging for the driver to back out and get turned around. The smaller Willys could easily be steered beside the Ford, and could escape without having to back up.

"Perfecto," said Grover, flicking on his battery-powered spotlight. "They're petting up a storm in that one." He killed the headlights and pulled next to the Ford. Perry swallowed hard and cranked his window down.

The Ford's windows were thoroughly steamed. The spotlight's rays barely penetrated the gloom revealing two vague shapes entwined in the back seat.

Perry took a deep breath and screamed, "Emergency! A killer-rapist has broken out of jail! We just saw him. Help! Open up."

The prey sat up and rolled his window just a crack.

"Nuts," grumbled Grover, "too small a target."

"What? Who are you?" shouted a voice from inside the Ford.

"Boy Scout Troop 149," Perry shouted back. "We're out warning people about the pervert-rapist."

"Did you say, 'pervert'?" shrilled a female voice. The Ford's back window moved down halfway.

"Bingo!" crowed Grover. Johnson raised up behind Perry and began spraying furiously. In his zeal he misjudged the shape of the Willy's rear window opening and unleashed a waterfall of crimson that splattered back inside the car. Instantly a stream of red liquid flooded the side of Perry's face.

"Dammit, Johnson!" screamed Grover.

"Ohmygod," shrieked the Ford's female as she spied Perry's gruesome appearance in the spotlight's beam. "Is that real blood!"

"Shoot straight!" yelled Grover.

"Now it won't spray," snarled Johnson.

"You have to pump it more for God's sake," beseeched Grover.

Perry groaned. "Let's get out of here."

"Hold it," said Johnson working the hand pump frantically.

"I've got it working now." A wet arc spewed from the Willys into the Ford's opening.

"What the hell?" said the male voice. "Ohhhh," whined the female voice.

"Okay! Mission accomplished. Awa-a-ay we go!" gloated Grover. He twisted the steering wheel violently and pushed the Willys gas pedal to the floor. Gravel flying, the squat little auto sped into the darkness.

"Think he'll come after us?" asked Johnson.

"It'll take him too long to get back in the front seat and get that big lunker backed out, "replied Grover. "He won't catch us. Not for all the tea in China. But just to play it safe, I'm going to drive clear around to the other side of the Butte. There's one more lover's lane down below the jail we can check out before we call it quits."

"Maybe we should just call it quits now," offered Perry.

"Don't be such a nervous Nelly. Now we've got our technique down pat, and if there's a car down this way, it'll take 'em forever to turn around after we make our hit." It was plain to Perry that Grover was gung-ho and turning him back now was out of the question.

Their next destination was a single lane, gravel road dwarfed by towering Douglas firs. "We're in luck," announced Grover. Ahead in the shadows was the outline of a single auto. Grover switched off the headlights and cranked the wheel hard so the Willys turned a quick 360 degrees. Then he backed down the road rapidly until the two cars were side by side.

"Geez, it's a Buick," said Johnson. "I recognize those little portholes on the side. Must be some old farts."

"So what. It just means we'll have bigger windows to shoot through."

Perry swallowed hard and began yelling: "Help! Help! The escaped pervert is after us. He'll be here any minute. Open up please!"

To the trio's surprise, instead of the window rolling down, the door of the Buick swung open and the dome light illuminated the couple inside.

Johnson immediately released a drenching red rivulet at the male figure. For a moment his face was obscured in a splatter of liquid. But as Johnson paused to pump, the man's features emerged distinctly. As Grover described it later, the man was clearly "pissed to the gills."

"Holy Toledo," gasped Perry.

"You ain't just a woofin'," murmured Grover.

"Let's get out of here. Now," gulped Johnson.

It was unmistakable. The man in the Buick was New Rose principal Barclay Beasely. And though Perry wasn't absolutely sure, he would have bet a lot of money that his female companion was none other than Francoise Redeaux.

Chapter Fifteen
More Rumors

Perry Palmer mumbled a half-hearted apology for getting home late for dinner and scrunched his chair up closer to the kitchen nook table. He picked up his tarnished fork from the oilcloth cover displaying clumps of bright red cherries and lush green leaves. He couldn't remember a time when there had been any other cover on that table.

His mother scurried from the gas range with their meal: left-over roast beef, boiled potatoes, boiled beets and day-old white bread from the Sunbeam Bakery Day Old Store. She opened the Frigidair and set a pitcher of milk beside his plate. "Well," she said, "What happened at school today?"

Perry sighed. Every night the same question. Did she think school was a continual source of amusement and entertainment?

"Mom, it was just like always. Nothing much happened. Nothing much ever happens."

"Well, I happened to run into Mrs. Fitzmorris at the Piggly Wiggly, and she said everyone at the school is talking about that Coach McIntosh."

"McIntosh? Do you mean McIntyre?

"McIntyre, McDonald, Macaroni, whatever. You know I have trouble with all those teachers' names. The point is she thinks he's acting scandalously, and I guess there was a big to-do about it at last night's PTA meeting. According to Mrs. Fitzmorris this Mcadoodle is acting like a wolf and flirting with the senior girls."

Perry filled his glass with milk splashing several large drops on the oilcloth. "Oh, boy," he thought. "They're really out to get Coach McIntyre now."

"Well, what do you think, Perry?" His mother pushed up the rimless glasses on her nose so she could focus on his face. "Is this coach some kind of drug store Romeo?"

"You know how Mrs. Fitzmorris is, mom. She's always on some kind of crusade. Coach McIntyre's okay. He just danced with some of the girls during noon break." Perry noticed that several bars of unwrapped Ivory soap were lined up on the nook's windowsill. His mother believed they lasted longer if left that way for several days.

She shook her head. "I hear it's more than that. I understand the PTA is going to petition to recall him."

"Recall him? You can't recall teachers. That's only for politicians and people who get elected."

"Well, maybe she didn't say recall. Maybe it was remove or reject. The point is they want him to answer for his actions. I'm surprised you haven't heard all about this. Don't you talk to anybody at school?"

"Sure I do, but nobody's said anything about this to me. I think the whole thing's getting way blown up. What's for dessert?"

"Chocolate pudding, and just for you I bought some Dreamwhip for a topping. It should be delicious *and* nutritious."

The next morning before first period, Perry sought out Johnson in the hall. "Have you heard what's going on with the PTA and Coach McIntyre?"

Johnson rubbed his upper lip. For the past month he had been trying to cultivate an Errol Flynn style mustache. To date he had produced only a thin fuzz. "I heard my dad and mom talking about it last night, but they shut up when I came into the room. It's my guess that somebody's out to get the coach, but good."

"But it's crazy, isn't it?"

"Who knows?" Johnson stopped rubbing his lip and stuck both hands deep into the pockets of his cords. "But I did see him and Amber Kelly walking together in the parking lot and they sure seemed to be enjoying each other's company."

Perry shook his head in disbelief. "Dang it, Johnson, this just isn't right. First, we have to hush up all we saw on Rocky Butte, and now McIntyre's getting railroaded."

"Hey, wait just a minute." Johnson scowled angrily. "Rocky Butte's a different kettle of fish. We agreed we couldn't do anything about that because nobody would believe us. Remember, you were the one who talked Grover out of calling up the radio stations."

"Yeah, but...."

Johnson grabbed Perry by his biceps. "We need more evidence before we can blow the lid off Beasely. You were the one who convinced us we had to wait."

"Okay. Okay." Perry sighed and rubbed his forehead. "But you can't convict a teacher just because he's seen after school talking to a cheerleader. We ought to do something."

"Yeah, like what?"

Perry shrugged his shoulders. "I dunno. Maybe go out on strike like John L. Lewis and the coal miners do. I heard somewhere that it happened once before at New Rose, in the old building before the War."

Johnson laughed. "Perry, old sock, that idea is dumber than dirt; capital D dumb. Besides, McIntyre has people sticking up for him. I understand some of the wrestlers are going to circulate a petition saying he should be rehired for sure next year."

As Perry mulled over Johnson's remarks, Kingfisher suddenly appeared in the hall and shouted, "Hey, you yahoos, take a look at what's going on out by the flagpole." He pointed toward the school's front entrance and hastily ducked back around the corner.

As Perry and Johnson approached the large, glass-paneled front doors, they could see that a small crowd of students had gathered outside in front of the flag-pole that had been "donated with pride by the New Rose H.S. Class of 1952." Several were pointing skyward and there was a steady buzz of animated conversation. Perry immediately spotted The Mouse on the edge of the throng aiming his 8mm-movie camera at the top of the flagpole.

"What's going on?" asked Perry.

"Take a look for yourself," replied The Mouse. "It's a scene deserving of an Academy Award."

"Oh boy," gasped Johnson. "Wait till Old Man Beasely sees this."

Perry squinted upward through his bifocals until his eyes focused on a baggy object swinging from the top of the pole. There was a crudely lettered sign on the object, which for a moment he couldn't quite read. Then he could make out the letters PTA. Suddenly, all became crystal clear: There, dangling from the New Rose flagpole was a likeness of Mrs. Fitzmorris, hanged in effigy.

February, 1955 News Flashes

Britain announces its ability to make a hydrogen bomb.

Comic books depicting crime and violence are banned from sales in Los Angeles.

President Eisenhower sends first "advisors" to aid South Vietnam government.

"Flying Saucer from Mars" by Cedric Allingham, a report on an alleged encounter with Martians, is published by the British Book Center.

Bill Haley's recording of Shake, Rattle and Roll passes the one million mark in sales.

★ NEW ROSE BUD ★

The Student Newspaper of New Rose High School

Volume XI, Number 6   *Friday, February 11, 1955*

Mr. Beasley Talks to Student Body

In a special student body assembly last Thursday, Principal Mr. Barclay Beasely told students that whoever was responsible for hanging PTA Pres. Mrs. Fitzwater in effigy was "up a creek without a paddle."

"We won't stand for this outrageous conduct," said Mr. Beasely. "And the sooner the hooligans confess, the better." He then threatened to cancel all dances, basketball games, wrestling matches, club meetings, and cafeteria snacks until the culprits were caught.

After an urgent plea from coaches McCready and McIntyre, Mr. Beasely later said, "Okay, I won't cancel the games and matches, but if we don't solve this crime in one week, I'm ready to cancel everything, like it or not." Anyone knowing who the hangers are is asked to contact the office.

BUD Staff Sponsors Special Record Drive

"A record a day keeps the veterans gay," was the battle cry during last week's record drive. The drive netted over 500 phonograph records which will be delivered to Veterans' Hospital on Sam Jackson Hill.

Chapter Sixteen
Hellnight

"You ready?" asked Johnson

"Yeah, I guess so," answered Perry. "Somehow this doesn't feel as much like fun as it used to." They were standing in the February night moonlight outside Kingfisher's garage. It was separate from the house and larger than most in the neighborhood. Kingfisher's dad had built it to serve both as a home for his Oldsmobile and as a sort of rec room. In the back he had installed a kitchen sink and some Formica-topped cabinets. He'd also framed in a closet-sized room containing a toilet, a small sink and a full-length mirror on the back of the door.

"Perry, you're just getting soft in your old age. We gotta make this a historic Hellnight for all of our club members to remember. Did you bring the bananas?"

"Sure. I gave them to Grover. He'll put them in the toilet." Perry shoved his hands deep into the pockets of his cords.

"Well, let's get going. Williams has already got the pledges in there and blindfolded." Johnson looked up at the moon and grunted. "We've got to get this show on the road and get out of here before Kingfisher's folks get home."

Perry opened the slender door at the rear of the garage and both stepped inside. Under the twin lights suspended from the ceiling were a dozen or more guys milling around, four with cloth blindfolds wrapped around their heads. Among the unmasked Perry quickly recognized Williams, Kingfisher, and several other members of the football team.

"About time!" hissed Williams from the corner. "You're fall president, Johnson, and you know we can't start without you."

"Oh, shut up," replied Johnson. He cleared his throat loudly and shouted, "Welcome, you sad and sorry pledges. For this is your night to be royally initiated into our great and glorious club, *Essex!* In all of New Rose, there is no finer brotherhood, no higher honor. Answer me, pledges. Do you have the courage to endure this initiation?"

"Yes," weakly chorused the four with blindfolds.

Essex had been part of New Rose H.S. since the early 40's. Originally it was roughly modeled after a college fraternity, but recently the faculty had cracked down on such secret clubs, and ruled that Essex could only continue if its purpose was "community service."

Naturally, the club leaders agreed, and the organization rolled on as before, except that annually members brought food baskets to needy families. Last year a parent complained to Principal Beasely about the club's disciplinary methods which centered around the use of a "hack belt," (it had inflicted some serious red welts on her son's behind), but it all blew over by graduation. There were three other similar "social/service" clubs at New Rose: *Ypres* and *Tisa* whose members were girls, and *Zeno*, the other boys' outfit. How the names came to be, or what they meant, was a mystery to current members.

"Excellent," barked Johnson. "The first step is to partake in Essex's special communion. Get down on your knees! Sergeant at Arms, come forward to administer the communion." He waved at Vernon Grover who walked toward the pledges, grinning fiendishly. In his hand he carried a large plate holding four oversized dill pickles which had been liberally coated with green chili powder.

"Open wide and take a bite," ordered Johnson.

Grover stuck a pickle in each mouth. "Bite down and take a big swallow," he said. "No spitting out."

Despite Grover's command, the pledges coughed, gagged, sputtered and gasped, with most of the pickle falling to the floor. Collectively, their faces were twisted into ugly grimaces.

"Geez, I hope they don't upchuck like last year's pledges," said

Perry to Williams who was watching with keen interest.

"This bunch's got stronger stomachs I think. Remember when the seniors did this to us?

Perry recalled it vividly. "I thought I was being poisoned. I was lucky I didn't toss my cookies right then."

"And that time with Pee Martin? He puked so much I thought we were going to have to use a blowtorch to clean the floor. He threw up every color in the rainbow. Boy, that was some night." Williams closed his eyes, savoring the memory.

Johnson, Grover, Kingfisher and the notorious Pee Martin had gotten the pledges back on their feet and were leading them toward the bathroom door. The rest of the group crowded behind.

"Okay," bellowed Johnson. "Now is the time you miserable pledges will dip your hands into the sacred ancestral bowl and bring forward the most glorious artifacts of our forebears. Awkward as this may seem it is traditional way of honoring our historic past. Pledges go forward and kneel before the divine bowl."

"Did you get some good, rotten ones?" Williams whispered to Perry.

"Yeah, they're really soft," said Perry.

"Outstanding!" said Williams. "And how about the manure?"

"It's on top of the tank and piled behind. Came from Rossi's farm. Cow and pig mixed, really stinky."

"Perfect," proclaimed Williams.

Once the four blindfolded Essex candidates were lumped around the toilet bowl, Johnson bawled, "Reach forward unworthy ones and grab the ancestral remains, and give them a good squeeze to insure you make the proper contact with the old ones."

From the pledges came cries of dismay:

"Yuck!"

"Crap!"

"Eagghhh!"

"Oh, no!"

Muffled guffaws escaped from the onlookers. Williams clapped his hands enthusiastically.

"Marvelous. Simply marvelous," announced Johnson. "Now for the final act of historic salvation and loyalty for mighty Essex. Take your prize from the bowl, grip it firmly and rub it all over the top of your head. You'll find it makes for a stimulating shampoo, and really fertilizes hair growth."

"Aw come on," bawled a pledge. "That's too much. That's sick."

"Rub it in. Rub it in!" merrily chanted the onlookers. "It's like the Brillcream ads," someone shouted. "A little dab 'ill do ya!"

The pledge nearest the door screwed up his face as a gob of the stuff fell on the edge of his mouth. He made a spitting sound, and yelled, "Hey, this tastes like bananas."

"Alright, we do have one pledge with brains tonight," brayed Johnson. "And to show that we respect brainpower, you can remove your blindfold. But all the others have to keep them on, proof that they are not yet worthy of joining our esteemed organization. Now, all of us are going to march to the official Essex cars and we'll take a little jaunt out to the grand finale... " He paused dramatically. "of this unforgettable *Hellnight!* Those pledges who survive are destined for honor and acceptance into a special band of brothers."

Williams slapped Perry on the back. "A great start, don't you think? Are you going with us out to Rossi's farm?"

"I don't think so. I don't feel so hot," said Perry. "Sherwood's got the flu, and maybe I'm getting the same bug."

"I wouldn't miss it for the world," said Williams. "A chance to watch those sorry pledges rolling around in the pig slop. Plus, Funkhouser's mixed up some excellent fake blood. They should freak out big when we pour it on their heads." He smiled broadly in anticipation.

Kingfisher who had been unusually silent, ran up beside Williams. "Hey, I almost forgot! Merton's Drug store is open late tonight, and with a bit of luck we'll be able to stop off on the way and send in each pledge to buy a box of rubbers. It'll be an evening to remember when we're old and gray."

"Yeah, well, good luck," said Perry. He watched Grover flush down the banana remnants while others cleaned up the manure, and hung back as, led by Williams, the group spilled out into the night, herded the pledges into cars and raced off.

"I wonder what's wrong with me," thought Perry. "Last year I loved this stuff. Tonight it seems kind of dumb, like something redneck whites would do to colored kids in Mississippi." He kicked a pinecone into the street. "I just don't know. It seems like lately I can't figure out what's the right thing to do." He walked down the driveway, shoved his hands deep into his pants pockets, and headed toward home.

Chapter Seventeen
The Trap

Sherwood had asked Perry if he would hang around until after basketball practice. "I've got a peculiar request to make of you, and I can't converse about it in school," explained Sherwood.

"Why so mysterious?" asked Perry. "Is your dad getting arrested for embezzling?" Sherwood's father was some kind of big wheel at the local bank who annually spoke to the Social Economics class about the importance of a good credit rating.

Sherwood grimaced and fingered the cover of his trigonometry book. "Actually, it does involve my dad, believe it or not, but I can't engage in frivolous dialogue right now, so meet me in the parking lot, okay?"

After the buzzer sounded for the last class of the day, Perry strolled into the gym and divided his time between watching a practice scrimmage and trying to read some of his English assignment. His class was wading through *Macbeth*, and the scenes with the witches particularly intrigued him.

He noted the wrestlers were still running laps around the perimeter of the gym. A 98-pounder, Arnold Ziegler, had confessed that the team was behind the effigy hanging of Mrs. Fitzmorris, and as a consequence every varsity wrestler was ordered to run 1,000 extra laps and write a 500-word apology. At the rate of 50 laps a night, they would be running for days to come.

After practice was finally finished Sherwood emerged from the locker room; his thin hair still wet and matted from the shower. He waved at Perry to follow him outside.

In the dimly lit parking lot, they squeezed into the front seat of

Perry's Chev where Sherwood let out a long sigh. "I'm sorry, Perry, but my dad insisted I proposition you about this thing."

"What thing?" replied Perry who was beginning to lose patience. Why did Sherwood always take so long to get to the point?

"Well, you know my dad got coerced into this PTA committee that is investigating Coach McIntyre?"

Perry didn't know, but he nodded anyway.

"So, my dad and Kingfisher's dad have cooked up this insidious scheme to catch McIntyre in some felonious act and force him to resign. They're sure he's been seen parked up on Rocky Butte with one of the cheerleaders, probably Amber Kelly."

Perry grinned. "So these daddy-o's are set to ambush him some dark night?"

"That's the conceptual theory. Kingfisher's dad has this gargantuan old press camera, and they plan to take some flash pictures that'll hang McIntyre out to dry for sure."

Perry fiddled with the steering wheel. "Sounds goofy, but what's it got to do with me?"

"My dad thinks for this to work they need an incognito car to drive. Mr. Kingfisher's got this red Studebaker Commander, and we've got the green Hudson, and they say those are too big and conspicuous. They want a diminutive, older, dark car." He paused and licked his lips. "Like yours."

"Like mine!" Perry turned so abruptly he hit the horn. "Come on, Platy, why me?"

"I don't know. Maybe my dad likes you. Anyway, why not? They even offered gas money for remuneration. What would it hurt? Look at it this way: it would be a chance to engage in espionage." Sherwood folded his arms. "Well, anyway contemplate it. I said I would talk to you, and now I have. How about some motorized transport home?"

After dropping off Sherwood, Perry drove around the block and parked the Chev under an overgrown weeping willow. He pondered

Sherwood's strange request. He didn't care much for Mr. Kingfisher, but Mr. Sherwood had always been friendly, and had once helped him figure out why the Chev wouldn't start. Plus Mrs. Sherwood was terrific. She was always full of compliments: ("Ray, that's a lovely sweater you're wearing today. I'll bet all the girls think you look sharper than James Dean.") And she regularly offered an overflowing platter of oatmeal-chocolate chip cookies to visitors: ("Perry, have a couple more. After all, you're still growing.")

He didn't like the idea of sneaking up on Coach McIntyre, but he had to admit he was very curious about all the rumors surrounding the man. "Oh, what the heck," he thought. "Why not?" "It'll be better than sitting home bored stiff."

Friday night found Perry once again waiting for Sherwood in the school parking lot. The Thorns basketball team had just lost to the Tillamook Cheesemakers in overtime, 56-54, and Sherwood had missed a couple of crucial free throws. He was likely to be in a sour mood. Fortunately, Williams, Johnson and Kingfisher all had dates so they could care less what Sherwood was doing with Perry.

Perry wondered what time it was. They were supposed to meet the adults at 9:45 PM, and if Sherwood didn't hurry up, they would be late for sure. Another five minutes passed, and suddenly Sherwood popped out of the darkness, opened the passenger side door and tossed his gym bag behind the seat. "Let's get this dilapidated bucket of decrepit bolts on the road," he growled.

"Don't get nasty with me," retorted Perry. "It's not my fault you tanked those free throws."

"So, rub it in," groused Sherwood. "Even Bob Cousy misses now and then."

Ten minutes later they connected with the two fathers on a quiet street near Kingfisher's house. "Bully of you, Perry, "greeted Mr. Sherwood. "You won't regret helping your school's morals like this." He was a bespectacled man who parted his graying hair in the middle, a style that made Perry wince. The Sherwoods, father and son, took up positions in the cramped back seat without exchanging a word.

Mr. Kingfisher, whom Perry had never seen wearing an open-collar shirt, lodged his ample frame in the front seat beside Perry. Much shorter than Mr. Sherwood, his head seemed undersized for his bulky body. He had on his customary white shirt buttoned to the neck and was carrying a bulky Speed Graphic press camera, the kind frequently seen in newsreels with flash bulbs blazing. "Does this window roll down?" he asked gruffly.

"It'll work, Mr. Kingfisher," said Perry. "Just turns a little hard."

"Well, it better." Mr. Kingfisher grunted. "I don't want anything blurring my picture when we nab McIntyre with the goods."

Perry gunned the Chev down Shaver Street and turned uphill toward Military Road, the route that circled Rocky Butte. He cleared his throat. "How are you going find him anyway? There will be a bunch of cars up there tonight."

"Oh, we've got that pinned down," replied Mr. Sherwood from behind Perry's right ear. "Our reconnaissance committee tells us he'll be in a green 53' Ford coupe, Oregon license plate 69-591. We're going to nail this dime store gigolo once and for all."

"Right," echoed Mr. Kingfisher.

"Are you sure he's really going out with a rally squad girl?" asked Perry. He downshifted into second gear as they began to climb the grade. "I mean, you could be mistaken."

"Not a chance," boomed Mr. Sherwood. "We've heard from some very reliable sources that this McIntyre fellow is a Hollywood wolf of the worst sort. Slow down now, I'm beginning to see parked cars." He peered out of the small, angled rear window.

Perry squinted out the driver's side window. He didn't see all that well in broad daylight, and his sight was even more limited at night. He wondered if they really had any chance of finding the right Ford.

"There! Stop and point your headlights over there," thundered

Mr. Sherwood, "looks like a Ford coupe!" Perry braked and turned so the headlights brightly lit the rear of the parked vehicle.

"It's a '52, dad, and the license plate is erroneous, too," announced the junior Sherwood who had up to this moment uttered not a word since the New Rose parking lot. "Well, it was the right color, anyhow," huffed the senior Sherwood. "If this car had windows bigger than portholes you might actually see something."

The best views of the city lights were to be seen at the very top of Rocky Butte. As Perry drove slowly around, he counted at least a dozen cars angled so as to capture the most romantic vistas. There were a number of Fords, but none matched the exact description of their quarry.

"Oh, my aching back," muttered Mr. Kingfisher. "This is turning out to be a wild goose chase. Howard, I thought you said we couldn't miss." He turned and glared at Mr. Sherwood.

"Doggone it, George. He's got to be up here. Perry, isn't there another road that comes to the top?"

"There's the road down the back side, but the guard rail is so close there's hardly any place to pull off and park." He paused as he remembered the night in Grover's Willys. "There is a kind of lover's lane down below the jail that's pretty dark and bumpy."

"Well, why didn't you say so before, for God's sake," exclaimed Mr. Kingfisher. "Sounds like a perfect place for man like McIntyre."

Perry pointed the car in that direction while trying to recall what Grover said he was going to do this night. He hoped he wouldn't run into the Willys on a similar mission. And what if they should happen to encounter the Buick? Boy, wouldn't that be something if they found Beasely instead of McIntyre down here.

The gravel lane was just as he remembered, and once again there was only a single automobile to be found close to the dead end. As they approached, Perry could immediately see it was too small to be a Buick. He stepped on the high beam button and the headlights illuminated a green Ford Coupe, license plate 69—and the last numbers were too blurred for him to read.

"That's him," crowed Mr. Sherwood, grabbing hold of Perry's seatback. "Definitely," seconded Mr. Kingfisher, cradling the Speed Graphic.

Perry accelerated and then skidded the Chev to a gravel-spewing stop beside the coupe. Two figures raised up inside. Mr. Kingfisher cranked the window down with a vengeance and snapped the big camera's shutter. There was a blaze of light as the flashbulb fired. Acting with surprising speed, Mr. Kingfisher opened his door and darted out. He pushed in another bulb and flashed a second photo at point-blank range into the Ford's interior. "Gotcha," gleefully shouted Mr. Sherwood from the backseat.

Mr. Kingfisher, now flushed with apparent victory, yanked open the Ford's driver-side door.

"Okay, McIntyre. The jig's up," he bellowed.

The dome light on the Ford's ceiling was flickering, but even in the dim light Perry could clearly see the face of the girl and her unbuttoned blouse. But it wasn't Amber Kelly. Even without her glasses, it was unmistakably Heather Breckenridge, the plump daughter of New Rose School Superintendent Harley Breckenridge.

"Holly cow," said Sherwood junior.

"Double and triple that," muttered Perry. He now could identify the man in the front seat. It wasn't Coach McIntyre. It was Lars Gudmonson, the school's newly-hired, youthful janitor

March, 1955 News Flashes

First FAX (radio facsimile transmission) sent across continent.

The Academy of Television Arts & Sciences announces EMMY winners for the past year:

Best daytime network show: "Art Linkletter's House Party."

Best variety show: "Disneyland."

Best audience participation show: "This Is Your Life."

Best situation comedy: "Danny Thomas-Make Room for Daddy."

On the Waterfront wins academy award for best motion picture; Marlon Brando wins Best Actor; Grace Kelly wins Best Actress.

Ballad of Davey Crockett by Fess Parker climbs to #1 in record sales.

US Air Force unveils a self-guided missile.

★ NEW ROSE BUD ★

The Student Newspaper of New Rose High School

Volume XI Number 7   *March 4, 1955*

Students Urged To Be Athletic Supporters

"Not enough students turn out for home contests!" This was the loud comment from both Varsity BB Coach Skeeter McCready and Assistant Varsity Wrestling Coach Rod McIntyre.

They added that some students didn't even have enough spirit to yell at Pep Assemblies held during school hours. "Disgraceful! It's Un-American," declared Coach McCready.

Seniors Prepare Special assembly

"Bodacious entertainment" is promised for the annual Senior Class Assembly next week.

The Senior girls trio will sing, "Lonesome Polecat," and "Let Me Go Lover." A tuba duet will be performed by Vernon Grover and Oliver Hill, and a dance routine will be forth-coming from Violet Rasmussen. Dirk Winslow playing his guitar and a tumbling act by several wrestlers will conclude this far-out display of talent by the "Class of '55."

New Janitor Welcomed

Students have been asked to give a friendly hello to our new custodian, Mr. Fred Rodinsky. He is replacing Lars Gudmonson who has "moved on to greener pastures," according to Principal Beasely.

Chapter Eighteen
Hoops

The second weekend in March found the Thorns' bedraggled basketball squad involved in the district playoffs at Gresham. Eight teams were competing for a berth at the State tournament in Eugene, and while the Thorns' chances were slim at best, Coach Skeeter McCready told an *Oregonian* sportswriter, "You never know, we might just sneak up on some teams like the Japs did at Pearl Harbor!"

To the amazement of both fans and foes, the Thorns won their first game, 54-52, when Williams tossed in a wild jumpshot as the final buzzer sounded. It was deemed especially surprising because the school they edged, Columbia Prep, had trounced the Thorns in the regular season. "Just call me,' Lucky Pierre!'" yelled Williams as he ran off the court.

Lady Luck stayed on the Thorn's side for their second contest as well. The team they were supposed to face, the Madras White Buffaloes, was forced to forfeit when it was discovered they had suited up two ineligible players.

Now the Thorns faced the daunting task of playing the lead-leading Gresham Gophers in the Saturday night final, and Perry, to his considerable surprise, found himself involved in the contest. That morning he had received a pleading phone call from Sherwood.

"Perry, you got to help us out tonight," bellowed Sherwood. "Bellhoffer's got the trots something awful."

"So what," replied Perry. "Bellhoffer's just the manager. You can get somebody else to hand out towels."

"Yeah, but he's also our official team scorekeeper. That's where we need you, Perry. I told Coach you'd be excellent for the job 'cause you did it before when we played JV." Sherwood sounded almost desperate. "Hey, I'll appeal to your penurious side. You'll get a great seat without having to buy a ticket."

So that evening as the two teams shook hands prior to tip-off, Perry found himself looking on from the long, wooden official scorers' bench positioned exactly at mid-court. A sea of howling, clapping humanity surrounded him, the official timer, the Gophers' scorekeeper, and a couple of reporters. The bleachers were crammed to capacity, and the Gophers' fans, enjoying the home court advantage, outnumbered the Thorns' supporters at least two to one.

Despite the Thorn's upset of Columbia Prep, they were decidedly underdogs for this matchup. The Gophers had won twelve in a row to end the regular schedule and had pulverized the Thorns in their two previous meetings. At Friday's pep assembly Perry overheard the Mouse predicting a blowout. "Our butts will be waxed," he proclaimed to a sophomore. "If it's closer than 20 points, it'll be a miracle."

Perry thought it wouldn't be all that disastrous, but had to admit an upset was extremely unlikely. "We can beat those guys," Sherwood had said over the phone. "We just need a couple of breaks."

"Oh, sure," said Perry. "You mean you need Elwood Adams to break his neck." Adams was the Gophers' star center, a slippery, six-foot-five, pimply beanpole who could hit soft hook shots with either hand. It was rumored that college coaches were camping out in his neighborhood.

In addition to Williams and Sherwood, the Thorns' starting five consisted of two pint-sized guards, Archie Mickleson and Art DaMonte, plus a red-haired transfer from Hawaii named Lloyd Dishender. The subs, like Kingfisher who generally spelled Sherwood, rarely played more than a few minutes unless the game was out of hand.

Because of their lack of height, the Thorns played a wide-open, gym rat kind of offense, fast breaking at every opportunity, and firing up shots from all angles. "We like to play like our hair is on fire," Williams had explained to Perry. They had won ten games during the season while losing ten, a better-than-average record for the school, but only the most rabid fans thought New Rose had a chance of making the State Tournament.

Both teams were so cold in the first quarter; Perry hardly penciled anything in his scorebook. At the end of eight minutes, Gresham led only 9-7, and even the heralded Elwood Adams was missing his share of shots. The second period was not much better. The Gophers managed to stretch their lead to 21-16, when just before the buzzer, Williams lofted a crazy, one-handed running shot that missed everything— rim, net, backboard—and Coach McCready screamed from the bench, "pass the ball, you nincompoop!" while the Gopher's student section began chanting, "Air ball! Air ball!" Archie Mickleson, attempting to retrieve the ball, dove on the floor and knocked the feet from under the much-taller Adams who crashed in a sweaty heap on the hardwood. "Geez, louise," thought Perry. "This is getting ridiculous."

Immediately, a middle-aged fan sitting almost directly behind Perry leaped to his feet and screamed, "Dirty foul! Come on, ref; throw out the little pip squeak! Rotten, dirty runt. Give him the thumb. Booooo!"

Perry winced. "Come on, buddy," he thought. "Don't get carried away. That's just the way Mickleson plays. He's always diving for loose balls and getting floor burns. He's about as dirty as Florence Nightingale."

"He deliberately tried to hurt Elvin!" continued the man. "He knows that's the only way he can win. Little thug. Send him home." A motherly-looking woman sitting next to him tugged at his sleeve and said, "Watch your blood pressure, George." He yanked his arm away and scowled at her. "I'm watching a dirty player, that's what I'm watching!" he snarled and sat down.

Perry silently fumed. "What's wrong with this yahoo?" he thought as he jotted down Mickleson's foul in the spiral-bound scorebook. "Why are some adults such jerks?"

Out on the floor, Adams, limping slightly, marched to the free throw line where he smoothly made both ends of a one and one. The Thorns quickly inbounded the ball and DaMonte tried one last frantic shot as the half ended. The ball clanked off the front rim, coming so close to going in that the crowd collectively held its breath for a split second.

During the break between halves, the rival rally squads took turns showing off their most involved yell routines, and the two school's pep bands attempted to inflict permanent damage on the spectators' eardrums. Perry couldn't help noticing when Amber Kelly leaped high, waving her pom poms; her sweater curled up revealing a bare skin midriff. He also noted that her long blond hair made quite a contrast to the more sedate pixie cuts of the other rally girls. "I can sure see what somebody like Coach McIntyre could get interested in her," he thought.

Play continued to be erratic in the third quarter. The Thorns twice threw the ball away on fast break attempts, Sherwood was called for too many steps, and Williams missed two easy shots. Then Mickleson picked up his third foul by hacking the arm of a Gopher guard as he tried to tie up his opponent for a jump ball. In the ensuing scramble, both players crashed to the court floor, and Mickleson picked up a nasty scratch on his elbow.

"Boo! You little creep!" shouted the man sitting behind Perry. "Give him the thumb. Open your eyes, ref. Boo!" Perry felt his blood rising and pushed his pencil so hard on the scorebook he broke the lead. "This guy is a royal pain," he thought.

Problems also plagued the Gopher five. They failed to convert four straight free throws, were called for too long in the key, and couldn't seem to get the ball in the hands of Adams. Frustrated at their mistakes, they began to lose their composure, and elbows were flying under the basket. The quarter ended with Gresham still ahead, 34-28.

Sherwood banked in a field goal to open the last period, and the Gophers missed a tough outside shot on their first possession. Then with the Thorns' fans screaming their lungs out, Williams went on a tear. In rapid succession he scored with a driving layup, a jumper from the key, and a goofy, off-balance shot from the corner. Back on defense he knocked the ball loose from Adams and plunged headfirst after it, landing on the sidelines amid a shrieking pile of Gresham rally girls. Struggling back to his feet, he planted a kiss on one of the cutest, who turned beet red and tried to swat him with her pom pom.

The ref scowled, "come on, knock that off, kid," but didn't see the heavyset Gresham forward come up behind him with fire in his eyes. He screamed, "You miserable retard! Leave my girl alone!" And he took a big roundhouse swing at Williams, missed him by a foot and blindsided the unsuspecting ref. Mickleson ran up from the other side and tackled the forward. Williams shoved Adams in the chest, and Adams shoved back. The crowd screamed and began to throw things. Both benches emptied, and the coaches frantically tried to separate the now brawling players. Fights broke out among students, and several adults were seen yelling and pointing fingers at each other. The PA announcer's voice turned hoarse as he tried to yell above the din: "ORDER. ORDER. EVERYBODY SIT DOWN. PLEASE!"

Directly behind Perry, the red-faced man was on his feet and waving his fist in the air. "Dirty bums," he screamed. "Thugs. Kick 'em out. Dirty, rotten sewer rats!" He turned to his wife, "Cheaters! That's the only way those dumb bunny Thorns can hope to win. Bunch of teen-age jerkoffs. Bunch of..." Perry could take it no longer. He could feel his blood rising uncontrollably. A surge of rage gripped his throat. He leaped to his feet, turned and pushed the man hard in the stomach right above the belt buckle. "Jerk, yourself!" yelled Perry.

The man grunted, "ooof," and sat down, looking as though he had just swallowed something inedible. His wife screamed and covered her face with both hands. "For God's sake, kid," said the man sitting next to her. "What do you think you're doing?"

"You're dumber than squat, you jackass!" shouted Perry. "Harelip blabbermouth! Big fat, stupid, idiot! You slimy, spastic queer." He struggled to spit the words out and stumbled backward when someone grabbed him by the arm and spun him around. It was Kingfisher, who had leaped up from the Thorn's bench when the melee began, but had run over by the scorer's table to avoid any potential bodily harm.

"Take it easy, Perry!" cried Kingfisher. "You want to get kicked out?" Perry sat down hard and sucked in his breath. One fist was still clinched. It took a couple of minutes for his anger to subside. Out on the floor, the coaches and refs managed to separate the two teams and herd them back to their respective benches. Kingfisher patted Perry on the back and scooted back across the floor. The officials then huddled at mid-court and came to the scorer's table to announce offsetting technical fouls. With pressure mounting, each team missed its penalty free throws.

The clock was reset to show 2:58 remaining, and the scoreboard now proclaimed the score to be knotted at 34-34. Perry stared straight ahead. He wondered what the man behind him was doing, but he didn't want to sneak a look. At least the guy was silent for a change. He wondered if he should make a run for it when the game ended. Once again the crowd noise reached earsplitting decibels, and threatened to raise the roof of the old gym.

On the court Williams was dribbling furiously toward the basket, and Elwood Adams was moving to block his path.

Suddenly it was as though a black curtain had been rung down on the stage occupied by the players and fans. It took a moment for the shock to settle, and then everyone realized what had happened. Something had caused the power to go out.

The cavernous gym went dark as a mineshaft. The crowd groaned, and Perry slipped out of his seat and made a bumbling scamper for a back door. He figured that if they got the lights back quickly, somebody else could finish scorekeeping. If he made a move now, he could avoid any further problems with the fan behind him.

The lights did not come back on, however, and soon, over the PA, it was announced that the game's conclusion was now rescheduled for the following afternoon. Happily and surprisingly, the fans in the inky gloom did not panic, but simply groused and swore as they stumbled over each other in an effort to reach the exits. Later it was learned that a utility pole transformer had been shorted out by some rambunctious squirrels who were instantly fried for their toothy misdeeds.

Ultimately, on the next day, the Thorns lost in overtime as Williams fouled out, and Adams regained his shooting touch. Perry, frequently looking over his shoulder, returned to finish the scorekeeping without incident. His adult adversary had disappeared.

"Heck of a game, wasn't it?" said Kingfisher at lunch the following Monday. "If the power hadn't failed, we might actually have won the thing."

Perry nodded. "I was just glad to get out of there alive. That guy I pushed was way bigger than me. I was out of my gourd."

"Yes, you were," agreed Kingfisher. "But be of good cheer. I understand that Mickelson's mother heard what you did and is going to call Beasely and tell him that you're an outstanding young man. For once you're luckier than Williams."

Chapter Nineteen
Mad Friday

A 20-year tradition at New Rose H.S. was "Mad Friday," a special assembly put on annually by the Letterman's Club. Generally it consisted of a series of corny skits and an occasional musical number. Because the skits frequently took pot shots at faculty and administration, Principal Beasely had threatened to cancel the event, but bowed to pressure from the coaches who insisted "it was a good way for our boys to blow off a little steam."

Perry was also wishing it might be canceled this year but for entirely different reasons than the principal. In a moment of weakness he had volunteered to head up the program committee and soon discovered that his committee mates expected him to take care of everything.

The four others who signed up, supposedly to help him, were Danny Williams, Vernon Grover, Ernest Funkhouser and to Perry's considerable surprise, Eddie "The Mouse" Fletcher. The Mouse hadn't attended any of the Club's earlier meetings, and Perry had forgotten that he had somehow earned a letter, but for what? "For managing the cross country team, you numbskulls," was the way the Mouse later informed everybody.

Perry couldn't believe it. First, the Mouse joined the Camera Club and now he was on the Mad Friday committee. The guy was turning into a social butterfly.

When the committee met, The Mouse's motives for joining the group quickly became apparent. He wanted to stir things up in a big way with the faculty. He was the only one of the quartet who actually offered new ideas for the program, but most of The Mouse's suggestions were far too bizarre to use. First he had urged Perry to bring a wheelbarrow full of water balloons on stage and then to lob them randomly into the audience.

"That'd get old Beasely's attention for sure," he snickered.

When Perry pointed out, "It might get us expelled as well," The Mouse shrugged and suggested that they bring a box of stray cats and release them on stage together with several large mongrel dogs. "With a bit of luck the cats will head right for the front row where all the teachers are camped out."

Perry was pretty sure The Mouse was just floating these ideas to get some yucks from the other guys on the committee, but he was worried that The Mouse was serious about the smoke bomb.

"It would be simple to make," explained The Mouse. "I've got a recipe I found in one of my dad's books, and we should be able to get the ingredients at any drug store. It won't kill anybody or anything like that; it just would create this huge cloud of black smoke that everybody would remember."

Perry had tried to talk him out of this stunt, but it didn't help that both Williams and Funkhouser were backing The Mouse's plan.

"Don't worry, Perry," said Williams after a particularly chaotic and unproductive committee meeting in Coach Gunderson's home room. "So we stink up the place. Who cares? Nobody expects the Lettermen to do anything brainy. It's just a chance to get out of class for an hour."

Perry also had to muzzle Grover who called him at home to argue for a Rocky Butte Lover's Lane skit featuring "a make-out artist who was obviously Principal Beasely." "No way," said Perry. "We've got to keep the lid on what we saw that night until we have some concrete evidence. Otherwise our ass is grass."

In desperation as the date neared, Perry decided on a three-pronged plan of attack: he wrote a couple of skits and recruited some reluctant sophomores to act them out; he talked Grover and Oliver Hill into performing a tuba duet; and he laid down the law to Williams, Funkhouser and The Mouse. "I don't care what you do," screamed Perry at the trio, "just do something! I'm putting you down for acts four and five, and if you don't come up with anything, you can just stand on the stage and pick your noses."

So when the designated Friday, March 18, 1955, arrived, Perry was a bundle of nerves. He still didn't know exactly what his tardy trio had in mind. They had all talked about having a full-bore rehearsal, but for one reason or other it never happened. The assembly was scheduled for immediately after lunch period, giving Perry and the other involved lettermen a last chance to get ready, but as the minutes ticked down, confusion was rampant backstage.

Kingfisher, as student body president, was supposed to lead the flag salute and introduce Perry as MC. As usual he didn't show up until the last minute.

"All set to go?" beamed Kingfisher as he suddenly pushed through the crowd backstage.

Perry stifled the urge to punch him. He took a deep breath and surveyed the scene. Grover and Hill, programmed as the first act, were tuning up their tubas, two chunky sophomores were tying on cardboard "armor" for their "Two Brave Knights" skit, and Funkhouser, Williams and Archie Mickleson dressed as cancan girls were stuffing grapefruits and balloons into their blouses. The Mouse was nowhere in sight and several other lettermen were arguing loudly about the movie director skit. From the other side of the curtain came the sounds of students filling the auditorium, scraping the folding chairs, giggling and talking, the steady hum of adolescent energy.

"I guess we're as ready as we'll ever be," answered Perry.

"Great," gushed Kingfisher. "I'll get things started. Break a leg, as they say in the theater." He stepped in front of the curtain and asked the audience to stand for the Pledge of Allegiance. Afterward, it occurred to Perry that the flag salute and one skit were the only parts of the assembly that came off without a hitch.

The tuba duet started off promisingly enough with Grover and Oliver belting out a passable "*Old Macdonald Had a Farm.*" Rather than quitting while they were ahead, however, they immediately launched into an encore number, "*Stars and Stripes Forever,*" and got badly out of synch. Grover compounded their debacle when one of his finger valves stuck, resulting in a sound much like a cow passing gas. They finished by storming off-stage in a mutual huff.

Trying to restore some control, Perry quickly ushered on the Two Brave Knights in their cardboard "armor." The skit was intended to parody the days of King Arthur's Court where one of the knights, Sir Lanceless, challenges the other, Sir Foppingham, to a duel. They quickly break their wooden swords over each other, and then resort to old-fashioned can openers to finish the battle. The cardboard armor is tied with string, so in fairly short order the knights can be reduced to staring at each other's wildly colored long underwear, the sight of which is supposed to be so shocking they will flee the struggle yelling, "I give up. I can't stand to look at anything so awful."

As the skit concluded, Perry couldn't understand why a number of senior girls in the second row were shrieking hilariously and pointing at Sir Foppingham, played by sophomore Cody Griswold. Then he saw why. Sir Lanceless' can opener had carved more than string and cardboard. The sharp point had severed the button on the trap door of Foppingham's long johns and exposed a sizable patch of white skin on his behind. From his perch on the corner of the stage, Perry could now clearly see Beasely frowning ominously in the front row.

Next, the cancan act with the three guys kicking and prancing had the audience howling, but mostly because William's grapefruits kept falling out of his low-cut blouse. He scrambled to pick them up while still kicking Cossack style and fell flat on his back. Mickleson, who had been trying some ballet-like pirouettes in his routine, tripped over Williams and crashed forward so the balloons in his blouse exploded with a bang. Concurrently the off-stage phonograph needle skipped on the cancan record with an ear-scathing *scraatch*. Perry yanked the curtain down to end the melee, and frantically signaled the movie director skit team to get on stage.

Standing in the wings and holding his head in anguish, Perry was startled by the sudden appearance of The Mouse who appeared very pleased with himself.

"Relax, Perry, it'll all be over soon." The Mouse was grinning and flashing his yellowish teeth. He was wearing a black motorcycle jacket. "And don't worry about the smoke bomb. The dumb druggist at Merton's wouldn't sell me the chemicals. Something about maybe blowing a hole in the roof. What I've got is way better anyway."

"For God's sake, Mouse, what do you mean?"

"Monty and me and Alvin are going to do a Marlon Brando thing. It's far out. You'll love it." Perry could now see Monty Carpenter and Alvin Witherspoon in the backstage shadows. Monty also was wearing a black leather jacket and goggles. He was sitting on a kid's large tricycle painted silver. Alvin was dragging a huge burlap bag.

"It's a spoof of '*The Wild One*,' you know, the motorcycle gang movie?"

Perry took off his glasses and wiped the perspiration from them. "Okay. Okay. What's in the bag?"

"Chickens."

"Chickens! Are you nuts?"

"When one of the Brando-types calls the other a chicken, we bring out the *real* chickens. The crowd'll eat it up."

On the other side of the curtain the crowd was responding with raucous laughter to the Movie Director Skit. It called for a "movie director" to film scenes with a star "actor" and "actress." The actor's hick "double" stood by closely. Just as the star was about to be hit with a pie, a bucket of water and a fake baseball bat, the director cried, "cut!" and asked for the double. The poor dope then stood in and took the blows. Finally the director called for a kissing scene, and the double leaped eagerly forward, only to be told by the actor, "Sorry, old boy. I don't need your help now." He then proceeded to give the actress a big smooch.

There was a burst of applause, and the Movie Director Skit team ran off the stage. Perry felt suddenly lightheaded. He still had to decide about the Mouse's act. Maybe this wasn't really happening. Maybe it was just a strange dream. He felt trapped. "Okay, Mouse, go ahead. You guys are on. Just don't get us all thrown in the hoosegow."

"Relax, man. Relax." The Mouse waved at Monty and Alvin. Perry thought he heard a commotion way in back where the fire door was located. The Mouse bared his bad teeth and strolled confidently out to center stage. He began talking to the audience but Perry was too frazzled to follow what was being said. The Mouse snapped his fingers and Monty raced out of the shadows on the Silver Tricycle. He circled the stage and stopped with a wheelie in center stage. Loud laughter was coming from the audience. Perry peeked out from the wings. Maybe this would turn out all right after all.

The throaty roar of a full-sized Harley woke him from his brief pipedream. The engine noise caromed off the walls and ceiling and was seconded by the shrill sound of squealing tires. A whiff of exhaust fumes blew across the stage as the motorcycle charged into view. A scream issued from the second row, and a collective gasp from the front chairs. The heavy machine had difficulty navigating the stage's cramped dimensions. It slid sideways and the rear tire hung spinning over the front of the stage. There were more screams and a clashing of metal as folding chairs were knocked over by scrambling students and teachers.

The Mouse was still at the mike uttering his lines, but his words were lost in the melee. He turned and yelled toward Alvin who rushed onstage while opening his bag. In a flurry of feathers and squawking, four Plymouth hens and a rooster bounded out and proceeded to run amuck, pausing only to defecate. Perry looked on in disbelief. Principal Beasely was waving his arms and shouting for everybody to stay calm.

"This assembly is over!" he boomed out. "Everyone report to their next class. Now! The assembly is over!" His last words were hard to hear, however, as one of the hens flapped crazily from the stage and landed squarely on his shoulder.

April, 1955 News Flashes

National Academy of Sciences announces plans for a study on the effects of atomic radiation.

Former President Harry Truman denies rumors that he would be willing to serve as Adlai Stevenson's running mate in 1956.

Albert Einstein dies at age 76.

Salk polio vaccine declared, "safe, potent and effective." Shots begin to be given to school kids.

Congress orders that all US coins now must bear the motto, "In God we trust."

★ NEW ROSE BUD ★

The Student Newspaper of New Rose High School

Volume XI, Number 8   *Friday, April 15, 1955*

Boy's League Assembly Slated for April 22

The big day for the Boys League is coming up soon and the following acts tentatively are scheduled: A girl's trio from the junior high under the direction of Mrs. Fern Flanders will sing.

And speaking of singing, Carl Gustafson, who graduated from NRHS in 1946, and is now co-owner of the Rosy Refuse Collection Co., will return to his alma mater to do some fancy Swiss yodeling. Also Terry Thompson will give one of his drum solos.

"We trust this clean-cut assembly will make students forget the unfortunate problems connected with last month's 'Mad Friday' mess," said Principal B. Beasely.

Girls' League Hears Speaker

The GL meeting held in the cafeteria was highlighted by a guest speaker, Mrs. Oglethorpe from the Meier and Mulnick Department Store.

Mrs. Oglethorpe, who works in the Housewares Department, showed the girls samples of china, silver, and crystal, all in the best selling patterns. She said that dinnerware is made up of two kinds: china and earthenware "but it is not necessary to have china to set a nice table." She reminded everyone that her store gives S&H green stamps with each purchase.

Chapter Twenty
Trout Fishing

Trout fishing season in Oregon begins sometime around the third weekend in April, and opening day was something that Perry had always been dimly aware of. Every year there were numerous photos in the *Oregonian* of happy anglers—generally small kids or old men—grinning foolishly and proudly displaying their catch. Then, too, Both Williams and Sherwood were fond of fishing, and had occasionally tried to talk Perry into going with them.

But Perry had always turned them down. It never sounded all that interesting, and, besides, he didn't have any of the required gear. When his dad had been alive, they had talked a time or two about going fishing, but nothing ever came of it. By contrast Williams' and Sherwood's fathers were keen on the sport and had encouraged their offspring to go with them as soon as they were big enough to cast a line.

Williams' dad was so fond of the activity he would take off after work at the aluminum plant to fish for carp and bluegill in the nearly stagnant ponds between the railroad tracks and the river. Perry remembered Mr. Williams declaring, "Nothing calms me down like hooking a mess of bluegill. Makes life worth living." Perry liked Mr. Williams, who was a large, thick-necked man who walked with a limp from an old football injury, but he could not understand why he and his son had such a passion for rod and reel.

When the trout season opened in 1955, it again prompted Williams and Sherwood to nag Perry about going with them on a fishing expedition. They put the same pressure on Johnson and Kingfisher, but each had some excuse why he couldn't go.

"At least give it a try," coaxed Sherwood. "It will be a salubrious experience. Plus, it will give you a chance to forget about the Mad Friday debacle."

"Well, I'm sure in favor of that," said Perry. "I'm still amazed we weren't all suspended. It was bad enough to get Beasely's tongue-lashing. He really put us through the wringer."

"And I've got plenty of equipment to loan you," chimed in Williams, "although I can't guarantee any kind of slobbery experience."

"Salubrious is a perfectly good word meaning wholesome and healthy," replied Sherwood, "and it wouldn't hurt you two to expand your vocabulary to more than monosyllables."

"So, okay, I'll use more sil—lah-bulls," said Williams. "But in the meantime, let's pick a day to go do the deed. And, Perry, you can't go through life as a fishing virgin. It simply wouldn't be sah-lube-reeous."

"I guess," said Perry. "'So, when do you suggest we play this Izaak Walton game?"

"Next Saturday morning," answered Williams. "It'll be one week from opening day, and most of the really stupid fishermen will have decided to stay in bed. Right, Platybooger?" He pointed a finger at Sherwood.

"Okay by me," said Sherwood. "Where should we pursue our piscatorial prey?

"If you mean where should we go fishing, I vote for the Upper Sandy River," said Williams. "It'll only take us a couple of hours to get up there, and it could be hot. Perry, you'll love it. Guaranteed."

Seven days later, at 6:15 AM, Perry found himself yawning in Williams' driveway and wondering why he had bothered to show up. Sherwood had talked his dad into letting him use the Hudson, and he and Williams were busy cramming fishing gear into the trunk.

"How many flatfish you got?" Williams asked of Sherwood.

"Enough," said Sherwood gruffly.

"You sure? There are a lot of snags in the Sandy. We're sure to lose some." He turned to Perry. "These lures are surefire fishkillers, ol buddy. We should catch a washtub full by noon."

"It's all Greek to me," said Perry.

"Come on. Let's perambulate," said Sherwood slamming the trunk lid.

As the big Hudson rolled out of the driveway, Perry, slouched in the back seat, noticed for the first time that rain was beginning to sprinkle on the windshield. "For crying out loud, we're not going to fish in a downpour, are we?"

Williams leaned over the back of his seat and slapped Perry's knee. "Take it easy," he said. "You won't melt. This only means the fish will bite better."

"Right," agreed Sherwood. "A little precipitation doesn't mean you'll be subject to decomposition." He turned on the windshield wipers.

Grumbling, Perry shut his eyes and tried to catnap. Williams energetically tried to coax the car's radio into transmitting something other than static. Sherwood began whistling, *"She'll be coming round the mountain, when she comes, boys..."*

"Geez louise," thought Perry. "This could turn out to be a scene from an Abbott and Costello movie." The loud purring of the Hudson's Hornet's V-8 engine contributed to his drowsiness, and he dozed off.

An hour later Williams gleefully shouted, "Wake up Rip Von Perry! We're here. The banks of the majestic Sandy are within spitting distance, and I can smell buckets of trophy rainbows just waiting for our arrival. It's even stopped raining."

Perry peered out the side window. They were parked next to a typical patch of Oregon rain forest. The mossy trunks of towering Douglas firs dominated his view. Beneath them clumps of huckleberry and rhododendron grew wildly. Small flecks of white were falling from the darkened sky. "For God's sake, Williams. That's snow!" he exclaimed.

"Hey, at least we got rid of the rain. Don't worry. It can't last, right Sherwood?"

"Indubitably," said Sherwood, pulling on a wool stocking cap.

"Meteorological phenomenon are common this time of year. Let's get rigged up." He yanked open the driver's side door, and stepped out. Williams followed suit on his side. Perry remained shivering in the back seat for a few minutes, then reluctantly joined them. He was happy to note that the snow did not seem to be sticking to the car.

"You'll love this gear," said Williams, thrusting a rod into Perry's hands. "Equipped with the latest in open-faced spinning reels, and the best in monofilament lines, no less. Easy to cast, a delight to reel in. Armed with this weaponry you've got it made to limit out by noon."

"Quit pontificating," said Sherwood. "What do you have for Perry's feet?

"Why, nothing but the finest in hip booties, to be sure," answered Williams, and he tossed a pair of wrinkled, rubbery boots at Perry.

"Are you sure these will fit?"

"Close enough, and beggars can't be choosers."

Perry tugged on the boots over his jeans and tied the rubber straps at the top to his belt. The boots were too big in the feet but otherwise felt okay. "Could be worse, I guess," he said.

"Off we go into the wild blue yonder," bellowed Williams who had donned chest waders, which made him look like a rubberized department store mannequin.

"Yeah, let's shake a leg," agreed Sherwood as he locked the Hudson's doors.

"Which way?" asked Perry, and he glanced upward at the sky. The mixed snow and rain continued to fall, but by now the day was much brighter, and it looked as though the sun was struggling to break through.

"Follow me, me hearties, and I'll lead you to the land of plenty," cried Williams, and to Perry's surprise, the ebullient Williams quickly found a faint trail leading through the woods.

"Dang Williams thinks he's Lewis & Clark," muttered Sherwood.

"But don't despair, Perry. We'll be on the river posthaste."

The trail wound downhill, and Perry soon realized that the muffled roaring sound he heard, was not the wind, but the noise of the river running.

"I haven't fished here before," Sherwood said to Perry. "But Williams says it could be splendiferous, and that we should have the place all to ourselves. Sounds like an exaggeration to me, but I figure it's worth a try."

"All I know, man, is I hope it warms up," said Perry.

"Just wait till you hook one of these lunkers," said Williams. "You'll forget all about whether you're hot, cold or upside down."

When they reached the river Perry had to admit it was a great example of Mother Nature at her best. The icy green water spilled over mossy rocks and formed shimmering, jewel-like pools. At intervals, decaying logs lay half-submerged in the water, and Williams said trout loved to hide in their shadows. It was deeper and faster than Perry had imagined, and more difficult to navigate, as the rough trail was hard to follow along the stream bank.

Williams and Sherwood confidently waded out and began casting their lures—flatfish for Williams and a Super Duper for Sherwood. Perry followed clumsily and tried to imitate their technique with his own gray-spotted flatfish. On his third cast he snagged a floating tree branch, but by tugging frantically, was able to save his tackle.

The mixed rain and snow had ceased, but Perry still felt chilled to the marrow. In particular his feet seemed to be almost numbingly cold, and as he cautiously stepped over the sunken river rocks he noticed a slight squishing sensation. Gradually it dawned on him that William's loaner hip boots were leaking.

"Fish on!" screamed Williams, and he jerked his rod violently to set the hook. "Oh, baby, it's a monster!" Reeling furiously, he brought the trout close enough that he could scoop it into his landing net.

"How big?" shouted Perry who suddenly realized he didn't have a net and had no idea how he could capture a fish if he ever caught one.

"Must be 16 inches or more."

"Bushwah!" yelled Sherwood who was watching just upstream from Williams. "A classic example of prevarication. If that's a foot long, I'll ingest your waders."

"You're just green with jealousy," sneered Williams who stuffed his catch into a cloth pouch. Come on Perry, you're next."

In the next hour or so, Williams hooked and caught 11 rainbow trout, a white fish and two chubs. Since the limit was 10, he released one of the trout, but because he considered the others trash fish, he proceeded to smash them savagely against streamside boulders.

During the same period Sherwood caught five rainbows and one German Brown trout.

Perry in the meantime lost three flatfish, two spinners and a rooster tail, and finally caught one chub. He tried to copy Williams' every move and even waded out as close as him as possible, but to no avail. The crowning blow came when he slipped, stumbled and sat down clumsily in the river. The water that quickly filled his boots felt as though it came directly from the North Pole. As he scrambled back to his feet, his teeth began to chatter uncontrollably.

"Williams," pleaded Perry. "Let's bag it. Call Sherwood so we can get out of here before I turn into a Popsicle."

"Aw, Perry, how could you be such a bumbler? I was just beginning to enjoy myself."

"If we don't quit now," said Perry; "you can enjoy yourself treating me for frostbite."

"Yeah," shouted Sherwood who had waded into earshot. "We don't want thrombosis, rigor mortis or hypothermia to set in."

On the bank, Perry pulled off and drained his boots and rung out his socks. He felt miserable from the waist down, but realized the only thing to do was to grit his teeth and get back to the car as fast as they could.

"I've got a spare pair of socks in the Hudson," said Sherwood. "Plus it's got a humdinger of a heater."

"Don't worry, Perry," said Williams. "If gangrene sets in, they can always amputate. You'll be a cool cat with a peg leg."

They hiked back through the woods, taking a different trail since they had moved a mile or so down the river in the pursuit of trout. Perry wondered if he could avoid coming down with a sore throat or worse, and hoped he could sneak into the house without his mother knowing about his chilled condition. He noticed that this trail was brushier than the other, but still relatively easy to follow.

Huffing slightly, the trio broke out of the forest and onto a rough, gravel road which Williams was certain would lead them back to their car.

"Hey, what's that sign say?" asked Sherwood, pointing toward a large metal sign facing the other way on a creosoted post.

"Dunno," said Williams.

As they passed it, Perry looked back and then did a double-take. In large red letters the sign proclaimed, "NO TRESPASSING! NEW ROSE CITY WATERSHED" and in smaller type, "violators will be prosecuted to the full extent of the law and subject to a maximum fine of $5,000."

Someone had scrawled "Kilroy was here" on the bottom half of the sign.

Sherwood saw it as well, and screamed, "Williams, you incredible idiot! Did you know about this?"

"Well, sort of. But nobody ever comes around here that I've seen."

"Good God, Williams," said Perry, "if we got caught, we'd be up guano creek without a paddle. How can you be so crazy?"

"Hey, no sweat, friends. Don't you remember how lucky I am? You're in like Flynn with me."

Later that night after Perry had sneaked back to his room and figured out a way to dry his clothes without his mother seeing them, he stared at the ceiling and said out loud, "Never again! My fishing career is over. Period." Then, silently, he thought, "Well, at least we didn't get nabbed by a game warden. And I don't feel like I caught a cold or anything, despite getting soaked. So, I guess I can just forget it even happened, sort of like a bad dream."

It was the next day, Sunday, before he noticed the itching on his arms. It got worse as the day wore on.

On Monday, he was scratching a reddish rash constantly all morning. "Oh, yeah," said Williams at lunch. "I guess the other day I forgot to warn you about all that brushy stuff."

"What brushy stuff?"

"Oh, you know," Williams paused and broke into a familiar grin. "Poison oak. Doesn't bother me, though."

Chapter Twenty-One
Perry's Quandary

Perry was in a sour mood. Here it was Friday night and instead of fooling around with his buddies, he found himself once again shivering in his front room and trying to please his mother.

For reasons he considered foolish, she had somehow managed to leave her wallet at work that day. She actually didn't realize it until Faith Galloway, who occupied the desk next to hers in the City Clerk's office, called around 7:00 PM. "Don't worry, dearie," she said. "I've rescued everything, and it's right here next to my phone waiting for you to pick it up."

His mother had been both embarrassed and relieved. "I just don't understand how I could have done that," she said. "I was showing Faith that senior class picture of you, and, oh fiddlesticks, I guess I forgot to put it back in my purse. Perry, could you please drive over to Faith's and get it before I have a nervous fit?"

So Perry had reluctantly agreed. To calm her anxiety, his mother sat on the sofa and began reading her favorite book, *Science and Health with Key to the Scripture* by Mary Baker Eddy. His mother's fascination with Christian Science had always puzzled Perry. For a time he tried to believe in it, but an incident when he was eleven convinced him that the religion's healing powers were highly suspect. He had been racing down Wygant Street on his Monarch bicycle when he hit a pothole at full speed and was painfully bounced off. In falling, his genitals were hammered by the bike's crossbar. "My nuts hurt like crazy," he later told his friends. His mother's solution was to call the Christian Science Practitioner and request that the proper amount of good, and healing,

words be recited for Perry. When that failed to produce any relief—
"Still thought I was going to be maimed for life," he recalled—Perry
made a lifelong decision that the theories of Mary Baker Eddy were not
for him.

He backed the Chevv out of their single car garage and looked at
the address his mother had given him. It took him a moment to figure
out that Faith lived way over on the north side of town. He had a city
map, but it was so wrinkled, he had a hard time making out the street
names. "What the heck," he thought, "if I drive in the general direction, maybe I'll get lucky." But nearly an hour later he discovered he
was driving in circles trying to find Faith's house.

"Rats, rats, rats," muttered Perry as he turned the Chevy coupe back
on to Intermountain Boulevard which at least was a well-lit thoroughfare.
At a stoplight he saw a neon sign high on a rooftop advertising the
Coon Chicken Inn, "Nationally Famous Coast to Coast." "Maybe
somebody there would know how to find Abernathy Street," he
said to himself, and pulled into the paved parking area in front of
the big restaurant.

Architecturally, the Coon Chicken Inn was more of a cartoon
than a building. The garish entrance was shaped like the huge smiling
face of a black man, or at least the stereotype of a black man. The whites
of the bulging eyes were backlighted, the fat lips were painted a blazing
red hue and parted in a gigantic smirk, revealing a mouthful of dazzling
teeth. A Pullman porter cap was perched at a jaunty angle on the head.
In the very middle of the mouth, lined up with the central incisors,
was the double door to the eatery. Perry had seen the restaurant only
once before when his Uncle Bob had taken him and his mother out for
a Sunday chicken dinner. His mother had remarked that the entrance
reminded her of an *Amos 'n Andy* radio show. She also had mentioned
that she was worried what the town was coming to, now that several
colored families had moved in. Perry couldn't believe anybody would
care. He parked the Chevy and trotted up the entrance. As he yanked

open the Coon Chicken Inn's toothy door, a heavily bundled couple approached on their way out. The man had his snap-brimmed fedora pulled low on his forehead, and his body shielded the woman from direct view. Perry pushed the door wide open and held it for them to pass, but his hand slipped and the door swung loose, bumping the man on his shoulder and knocking off his hat.

"Oh, geez, sorry," said Perry, and snatched back the door. He and the man both reached for the fallen hat, and for the first time Perry saw his face clearly. It was Barclay Beasely.

Perry stood up straight and blinked. For an instant his eyes met those of the somber principal. Than Beasely replaced his hat, turned abruptly and rejoined the woman waiting for him. Perry blinked again. In the streetlight there was no mistaking the striking profile of Francoise Redeaux.

After school on the Monday following his strange encounter, Perry told Johnson of the experience, and asked what he should do, if anything. At the same time he also let Williams and Sherwood know about the night on Rocky Butte in Grover's Willys. He explained that lately Grover seemed to have lost interest in pushing for an expose`.

"You got him by the short hairs," suggested Williams enthusiastically. "I'd ask for $10,000 and the scholarship." Unlike the others, who weren't out for spring sports, Williams was on his way to baseball practice. He was slightly late as usual, but happy to pause and offer his opinion.

"But I don't have any witnesses," sighed Perry. "It'd be just my word against his. And it happened so quickly it seemed unreal."

Johnson, who was leaning against a locker, nodded. "You have a point there, Perry old boy. It's just like that night with Grover. We knew it was Beasely, but how could we prove it? With our luck Beasely would have thrown us in the can for libel or slander, or..."

"Communist-inspired juvenile delinquency," hooted Williams.

"Yea, verily, hold your water," said Sherwood who was peering solemnly at his slide rule. "Give old Beasely sufficient magnanimous rope and maybe he'll hang himself."

So on Friday, when Perry's homeroom teacher, Mr. Brimmer, handed him the note asking him to stop by the principal's office after the day's last class, Perry's heart sank. What in the world did Beasely have in store for him?

Nervously he made his way to the front of the building and the entrance to Beasely's quarters. An oversized, glass-topped, oak desk dominated most of the principal's office. It was so large Beasely had to turn sideways to slip by and reach his high-backed leather chair. Other than several plaques on the wall and a framed photograph on his desk, there were no personal touches to be seen. Beasely prided himself on being a no frills administrator, one favoring the lean and mean school of principalship. He did not, however, exhibit the same pride in his personal appearance. The principal was wearing his usual dingy brown suit, and his favorite necktie which featured oddly colored flowers and a prominent stain.

During the year Perry had noted the stain and idly wondered what had caused it. Gravy? Grease? Booze? Kitten poop? He'd heard Beasely had pet cats. He finally gave up guessing.

"Have a chair, Palmer," boomed Beasely. "I hope you're having a productive senior year."

"Yes, sir," meekly replied Perry.

"You know, Palmer, I've been looking over your records, and I see that you've applied for the Mortimer Woodhall scholarship."

Perry gulped. It was a long shot, but if he won that scholarship, he could afford to go downstate to the university rather than being stuck at home and forced by economics to enroll at a lesser college in town.

"Well, yes, I guess so. I don't know if I have much of a chance." Beasely leaned back and clasped his hands behind his head. "You might have more of a chance than you think, my boy. You know I'm chairman of the committee that awards the Mortimer."

Perry swallowed hard. He had heard that Beasely was someway

involved but he didn't know how. "How would that affect me, sir?"

"Well, my boy. I just might want to put in a very—let me emphasize very—strong recommendation for you. It all just depends." Beasely leaned forward and folded his hands on a small manila file folder lying in the center of the desk. Perry thought it had his name on the tab.

"Depends, Mr. Beasely?"

"Yes, *depends*, Palmer. I believe this scholarship should go to a student with special qualities. Oh, grades are important and yours aren't bad, but it's more than a grade average that's important to me. What I really value are those intangibles like," and here he paused to look directly at Perry, "loyalty, yes, loyalty, and the ability and talent to keep confidential matters *confidential*. You know, Palmer, in World War II they used to say, '*loose lips sink ships*', and that's so true today. Do you read me, boy?"

Perry nodded. So it wasn't any hallucination last week. That really had been Beasely and Francoise, and the principal sure didn't want the word to get out about his apparently intimate involvement.

"Yes, Palmer, as you go through life, I think you will quickly find that the ability to keep a confidence is worth its weight in gold, so to speak. It's an important lesson to learn, don't you think?"

"If you say so," answered Perry.

"Good. I'm glad you agree. Now, of course the scholarships aren't announced until graduation night, but I can assure you that it will be a pleasant evening for you and your mother. Now I'm sure that you can understand that our little chat has to be kept just between us, correct?"

"Oh, yes, I understand."

"Wonderful." Beasely stood up and this time clasped his hands behind his back. "Well, that's all for now, Palmer. Thanks for coming by."

Perry stood up and turned to leave. Over his shoulder he heard one last remark from Beasely: "Remember, Palmer, loose lips sink ships." It was the only time Perry had ever heard Beasely chuckle.

That night Perry tried to concentrate on his homework, but his mind kept wandering back to the meeting in Beasely's office. "So now what should I do?" he pondered. "I could really use that scholarship, but I hate to let old man Beasely get away with this Francoise thing. And, I'm not sure I trust him to actually come through on his promise." The phone jingled in the breakfast nook, and he could hear his mother answering in her Emily Post-approved voice.

"It's for you," she announced. "I think it's that Johnson boy." He walked through the kitchen, and she thrust the receiver at him.

"Don't talk too long. I know you've got homework."

"Is that you, birdbrain?" asked Perry.

"Whaddya mean birdbrain?" yelled Johnson. "This is your all-knowing, extra-wise, true-blue buddy. And I want to hear what happened with you and our esteemed principal. Is he going to pay you off?

"Well, sort of." Perry paused to make sure his mother wasn't trying to eavesdrop. He could hear her fiddling with the black & white TV in the living room.

"It's like this: if I shut up, he'll get me on the inside track for the Woodhall Scholarship."

"Hey, not bad," said Johnson approvingly. "Worth a few bucks and more. So are you going to clam up or call Walter Winchell or better yet, Hedda Hopper?"

"Doggone it, Johnson, I don't know what's best. What would you do?

Johnson cackled loudly. "Take the money and run, man! Don't look back."

"Yeah, but Beasely's such a greaseball. I hate to let him get away with anything."

"True enough, my boy. True enough." Johnson was silent for a few seconds. "How about this for an answer? Wait till graduation, and after the scholarships are awarded, quietly get the word about Beasely to the *Oregonian*."

"You mean, double-cross the bum?" Perry sounded uncertain.

"Hey, all's fair in love and scholarship wars," replied Johnson. "The guy deserves the worst. He's never played fair. Why should you? I say give him the classic shaft."

"Just because he's rotten, doesn't mean I am." Perry switched the receiver to his other hand.

"That's enough talking for now," cried his mother from the living room. Tell your friend you have homework."

"Hey, I gotta go," said Perry.

"Okay, I'm hanging up," said Johnson, "but remember these words of wisdom: If you don't know what to do, don't do anything. At least not until you've got that diploma in hand. Okay?" The phone clicked off.

Perry stared at the flowered paper behind the wall phone. Maybe Johnson was right. Maybe it would be best to wait till graduation. It was less than a month away, and Beasely's secret might leak out anyway. For certain, the Mouse was up to something. Maybe he would find a way to spill the beans. Perry's head was beginning to ache. "Okay, I'll wait," he whispered. "But I sure wish I could figure this thing out."

May, 1955 News Flashes

U.S. Supreme Court directs states to end public school segregation "with all deliberate speed," but refuses to set a deadline.

"Swaps," ridden by jockey Willie Shoemaker, wins the Kentucky Derby.

Variety Club in Washington D.C. presents its "Mother of the Year" award to Pat Nixon, wife of the vice president.

New York State Supreme Court okays the revival of burlesque shows in New York City after an 18-year ban.

West Germany becomes a sovereign state.

Pulitzer Prize for drama is award to Tennessee Williams for "Cat on a Hot Tin Roof."

★ NEW ROSE BUD ★

The Student Newspaper of New Rose High School

Volume XI, Number 9　　　　*Friday, May 7, 1955*

(Last Edition for this School Year!)

"Stairway to Stars" To Be Theme of Prom

"Stairway to the Stars" will be the theme of this year's junior-senior prom to be held from 8:00 to 11:30PM in the sunken ballroom of the Masonic Temple, May 14. Twelve adult chaperones have been selected.

"Have a good time," said Principal B. Beasely at last Friday's assembly.

He then reminded students that anyone caught necking, petting, smoking, cursing or breaking curfew, will be suspended or turned over to the New Rose Police Juvenile Department.

Scholarship Time

Seniors are eagerly awaiting news of the winner of the Mortimer Woodhall College Scholarship. Principal B. Beasely predicted, "It will be a student whom we can all be proud of."

Seniors Take Trip

The seniors took their annual trip to the state capital last Monday.

After viewing the Senate and House of Representatives students were fed lunch and then treated to a visit to the McLaren Reform School for boys.

Chapter Twenty-Two
A Claim to Fame

At last the final week of the school year arrived, and Perry decided he would watch Williams' last baseball game. Sherwood, Johnson and Kingfisher all said they would attend as well, but when the rain began to fall heavily around midday, they realized the contest would be washed out and made other plans.

Having nothing better to do, Perry wandered into the locker room after school and found Williams and his teammates all sitting on benches in full uniform, hoping that by some rain god miracle the game would still be played.

Perry had never been especially fond of baseball, and he was always surprised at Williams' enthusiasm for the endeavor. But if ever there was a natural for the sport, it had to be Williams who was batting .460 with a dozen home runs and a slew of extra-base hits. It was rumored that he was only a handshake away from nailing down a college scholarship. Perry found him over by the equipment cage, punching his hand into a well-oiled fielder's mitt. Sitting next to him was Hardy Klingberry, a pudgy kid with blond sideburns, who was the Thorn's catcher. He was still wearing his shin guards and chest protector.

"You guys are the eternal optimists," said Perry. "This game could only be played in submarines. That field is soaked to the gills."

"I know. I know," said Williams. "I walked out there a little while ago, and there was a puddle back of first base deep enough to drown a St. Bernard. I just hate to see it end. Don't you feel that way, Hardy?"

"Yeah, we didn't win all that many, but it was mostly fun." He started to remove his chest protector. "Plus, having this game rained

out is great for Kretchmer. It means his record is safe. He won't have
to bat again, and he's already told everybody he's retiring for good after
this season. In fact I think he's already dressed and gone."

Perry pondered the name, *Kretchmer*. He couldn't place him
right away but them remembered he was a transfer from some school
like Molalla, and that he was small, blond and kind of pigeon-toed.
Perry couldn't recall anyone saying he was much of an athlete.

"Yup," laughed Williams. "You're right for once. Gerald Kretchmer
will now go down into the record books."

"For what?" asked Perry. "He was never mentioned in the *Bud*.
You were the guy who got all the ink."

"Now that I think about it, it was really kind of amazing," said
Klingberry. "I mean we thought he'd never make the team, and when
he did, we thought he'd never last."

"Your telling me he wasn't much good?" said Perry.

"Much good!" laughed Williams. "He was awful, wasn't he Hardy?"

Klingberry nodded. "He might not have been the worst player
in the league, but he certainly would have made the top ten list. I still
can't believe the coach stuck with him."

"Well, he was a lefty, and we didn't have anybody who could
pitch from that side."

"He was a pitcher?" asked Perry.

"Tried to be," answered Klingberry. "But, God, he was wild. I
hated to try to catch him. You never knew where the ball might go. I
remember one time in practice I called for a curve, and he fired it right
over the backstop."

"That's why he never got in a game," chimed in Williams. "That
is, not until last week at Gladstone."

A puzzled Perry locked eyes with Williams. "So, what happened?"

"It was weird from the start. We had three guys out with the flu,
and there were errors galore."

"On both sides," added Klingberry.

"Yeah, then it went into extra innings, all tied up at 12 to 12."

"And in the top of the 10th, with two out, Dishender, our last good pitcher, loads the bases, then announces his arm is suddenly weak as a warm noodle, and he can't go on. I thought you'd end up pitching." Kingberry pointed at Williams.

"So did I. But, lo and behold, coach sends in Kretchmer."

"Yeah. I heard him say, 'I got a feeling.'"

Perry leaned forward. "So what happened?"

"He threw two pitches that were way wide and then got one over the plate. The Gladstone batter swung from his heels and really socked it. I thought we were dead meat."

"It was like a rocket," continued Williams, "and aimed right at Kretchmer. I thought it would take his head off, but he stuck up his glove in front of his face, and, ka-thunk, darned if he didn't hold on to it."

"Unbelievable," said Klingberry

"But that's not the best part," gloated Williams. "Not by a long shot. In the bottom of the 10th, coach realizes Kretchmer is going to have to bat. I'm first up, and walk on four pitches."

"Then you steal second."

"Yeah, in like Flynn. I'll bet I could have stolen third, too."

"Well, you didn't have to, 'cause Mickleson laid down a nifty sacrifice bunt and moved you over."

"But, then you struck out."

"Yeah, well, nobody's perfect."

Williams shook his head. "So, you know who's up next? Kretchmer, of course, and he hasn't been at bat in real game all year. And, even in batting practice, he was always whiffing."

"Hit left handed and had a swing like a rusty gate."

"I'm on third thinking it's hopeless unless I do a Jackie Robinson and steal home. And, right away, it's two strikes on Kretchmer."

"Then, he fouls one off."

"Right. But, on the next pitch he actually gets the bat on the ball.

He swings so late, the ball loops to the opposite field and falls just over the third baseman's head. It was duck soup beating the throw home."

"We win!" shouted Klingberry. "It was terrif."

Perry was still bewildered. "Okay, it's a nice story, but what this record you talked about?

Williams scowled at Perry. "You ever hear of Ted Williams?

"Of course. Who hasn't?"

"Know what he did in 1941?"

"What?"

"Hit .406. The last time any major leaguer has hit over .400. Some think that record will stand forever."

"What's that got to do with Kretchmer?"

"Here's what, you imbecile. Kretchmer's baseball record is one hit for one at bat. Do you know what that gives him for a batting average?"

Perry blinked. "Pretty good, I guess."

"l,000, that's what it gives him. One thousand! A perfect batting average for the entire season! And a clear-cut 594 percentage points better than Williams' best. Plus, it now looks like his statistic will stand as a perfect *lifetime* batting average."

"Kretchmer knows it, too," said Klingberry. "I heard him tell one of the JV's: 'Listen, kid, you better show some respect. I'm the only guy around who has out-hit Ted Williams!'"

Chapter Twenty-Three
Graduation

It rained early on the day of New Rose's graduation ceremony, but to the relief of Perry's mother, the sun poked through in the afternoon, and by evening everything was drying out nicely.

"Isn't it time for you to get going?" she asked anxiously. "After all, surely you don't want to be late for the biggest day of your life. And, aren't you supposed to pick up the Johnson boy or somebody like that?"

"Yeah, yeah. It's Johnson, and I'll go, but we've got plenty of time. We don't have to pick up our caps and gowns till 7:00 PM. "Perry ran his hand over his freshly barbered head. "And I guess you'll get a ride with Uncle Bob?"

"Yes, indeed. He and Aunt Darlene wouldn't miss this for the world. Uncle Bob is sure you're going to receive some big award tonight. I told him I thought you probably would get a scholarship to a college like Sanford or Linfield, or, maybe even,ULCA."

"Mom, it's *Stan*ford, and *UCLA*, and the odds of me getting a big time scholarship are currently slim to none."

"Well, don't be too sure, Mr. know-it-all," huffed his mother. "I think Mr. Beasely has his eye on you. Especially after you won that 'Voice of Democracy' contest."

"Mom, I didn't win that contest. I only got honorable mention for my speech."

"That's still an honor, and I'm sure Mr. Beasely knows it, so there." Perry's mother picked up her needlepoint, signaling that the conversation was over. "Now I think you should be on your way."

Perry carefully backed out of the garage onto Wygant Street, drove slowly the two blocks to 102nd street and turned right. Traveling a route he had taken countless times in the past, he passed Prescott Street where Williams lived, then Skidmore Street where Sherwood and Kingfisher resided, and swung left on Shaver, the road leading to the high school. He passed the outer edge of Maywood Park, the manicured neighborhood containing the DuPrey residence and Francoise Redeaux. No doubt she was right now putting the final touches on her makeup for the big night. Perry grimaced. Even now he still didn't know what to do. Should he have exposed Beasely and Francoise? But who would have backed him up besides Grover and Johnson? For sure his mother would have been embarrassed no end. And then there was the scholarship deal. But he really didn't care about that. He just wanted the whole business to go away. Still a small, nagging voice told him 'you've got to do something!' "Okay!" said Perry out loud. "Okay! I will. But, first just let me graduate."

Johnson was waiting on his small porch when Perry pulled into the gravel driveway. Normally Johnson would have driven his own car, but last week it had thrown a rod and now sat sadly up on blocks in front of the garage. He rapidly bounded across the lawn and yanked open the Chevy's creaking door. "Perry, old boy, can you believe it? We've made it! We're done! Soon we'll be living the life of Riley. Tonight we get the ol' sheepskin and tomorrow the world is our pigeon."

"Oyster," corrected Perry backing out cautiously. He saw Mrs. Johnson carefully watching their exit from the front window.

"Oyster, clam, octopus, whatever. The point is we're gonna *graduate*. I thought the day would never come. How long have we known each other? Sixth grade?"

"Yeah, fifth or sixth." Perry laughed. "Seems like forever."

Johnson fiddled with the buttons on the Chev's radio. Heavy static interrupted the Penguins rendition of *Earth Angel*. "I'll tell you what seemed like forever: Miss Graystone's senior English class. I thought I was never going to get out of there with all that Dickens and

Shakespeare stuff. Have you got the antenna all the way up? This radio doesn't work for beans."

Just ahead Perry could see the glow from the school's lights. He ignored Johnson's complaint about the radio. "What do you remember most about this year?" he asked.

"Went fast, didn't it? Seems like only yesterday we were pilfering golf flags and yanking up all those For Sale signs."

Perry smiled. "Too bad old Beasely didn't take the hint and move on."

"Bums like Beasely never move on without help. They have to be booted out. And, take it from your Uncle Johnson, that still could happen."

"Yeah, sure. Like tonight, maybe?" Perry shook his head.

"Don't laugh. I've got a feeling this isn't going to be an ordinary graduation night."

"I'll believe it when I see it," said Perry as he wheeled into the parking lot.

Graduation at New Rose always took place in the high-ceilinged auditorium/cafeteria. The lunch benches and tables were cleared away and replaced with rows of gray metal folding chairs. The first two rows were reserved for the 132 graduates. Off to one side, close to the cafeteria counters, was a grouping of chairs for the school band which had been drafted to play the national anthem. On the back wall, taped under the window of the audio/visual projection room, was a large paper banner reading: "Congratulations Class of '55!"

On the same elevated stage where Mad Friday had been enacted, several better quality folding chairs were arranged in a semicircle behind the podium. These would be occupied by the speakers: Principal Beasely, Superintendent Breckenridge, School Board Chairman Horace Finlay, Reverend Manly Hoffstedder, PTA president Mrs. Fitzmorris, Salutatorian Randy Sherwood, and Valedictorian Freida Lewick.

Mild mayhem was taking place backstage as the seniors jostled each other, struggling to put on their black and white caps and gowns. Miss Ringwater, the senior class advisor, was frantically trying to line the students up in alphabetical order and find out how many were missing.

"Has anyone seen Eddie Fletcher?" she shrilled over the din of 130 teen voices.

"Saw The Mouse yesterday at the camera store," replied Monty Carpenter. "Haven't seen him today, though."

Williams came up to Perry and whispered, "What's the latest with Beasely? Is he going to come through with your rooty tooty scholarship? Or are you going to blow the whistle?"

Perry rubbed his chin. "I'm probably cutting my own throat, but I've decided I can't let Beasely make me more of a coward than I already am. As soon as this graduation jazz is over, I'm talking to one of those Oregonian newspaper guys. Johnson and Grover will probably back me up. If that means Beasely kaboshes my scholarship, well, that's just tough shoes. Win some, lose some."

Williams nodded. "Good on you. I hope ol' Beaser-head get the firing squad for his Frenchy fun. Now remember, the party afterward is at Kingfishers, and we don't care if you have a date or not. Even Sherwood's coming. So be there or be square."

Perry muffled a laugh. "Good old Williams, the original party animal," he thought. "I wonder if Francoise will show up."

"Okay, class. Please listen up." Miss Ringwater was close to hysteria. "We need to start moving in to be seated in your chairs so please stay in alphabetical order. If you don't receive a diploma with your name on it, don 't worry. We'll straighten it all out after the ceremony. And girls, please, no gum chewing. *Boys!*" She frowned directly at Williams. "Keep your hands to yourself. Now let's go."

Perry trailed in to the now jam-packed room and took his assigned chair between Vesta Perriwinkle and Bernice O'Reilly. He noted someone had written in red ink, "Graduation's a gas" on the back of the chair in front of him. One row back sat Francoise who was to receive some kind of honorary diploma. He wondered where his mother and his aunt and uncle had found a seat. "Well," he thought, "at last it is really happening. I am actually going to get a diploma!"

Much to Perry's surprise, the opening moments of the ceremony came off like Swiss clockwork. Reverend Hoffstedder's invocation was blissfully short. Kingfisher led the pledge of allegiance without knocking over his chair, and the senior-less band tooted through the national anthem as though they knew what they were doing.

Principal Beasely welcomed everyone and introduced Superintendent Breckenridge who droned on for several minutes about the stellar qualities of this class due, no doubt, in large part to the hard work and dedication of the New Rose faculty and administration, not to mention the School board, the PTA etc. etc. blah, blah, blah. Perry's eyes were beginning to glaze over. He blinked to keep awake, and as he did so, for the first time noticed that the huge movie screen suspended from the ceiling above the stage was lower than normal. It had been donated by the Class of '53, and was the pride and joy of the Camera Club because of its size and reflective surface.

At last Superintendent Breckenridge cleared his throat and announced that it was his great pleasure to introduce this year's valedictorian, Freida Leiwick, who was a perfect example of the quality education one gets at New Rose High School.

Freida, who was so short she barely could be seen behind the podium, began to speak in her trademark high-pitched voice. "Confidently we face the future," she declared, "for we know we can build a better tomorrow, a stronger world where the bright light of our youthful energy can overcome the dismal darkness of......"

Abruptly, the auditorium lights shut off, plunging everything into startling darkness. With a loud clunk the big movie screen suddenly unrolled downward. The bottom whacked the top of the podium and nearly beaned poor Freida. A powerful light beamed out from the A/V projection room at the back of the auditorium. At once a bright, moving image appeared on the screen. On stage, Principal Beasely screamed, "Get those lights back on immediately!" but to no avail. In the audience, loud murmurs evolved into shrieks as students and parents began to recognize the figures on the screen.

The film was grainy and slightly out of focus, but there was no mistaking the duo shown. Principal Beasely was in his undershirt and leaning forward to give a big smooch to Francoise Redeaux. She, in turn, was dressed only in a frilly brasserie and panties. As soon as the kiss finished, she began a sensuous dance routine in front of a smirking Beasely who clapped wildly and appeared to be either singing or chanting. Superimposed on the screen were crudely lettered words reading, "Welcome to the Sweet Dreams Motel."

All rows were now in a frantic uproar. Adults were shouting, students were hooting and pointing, chairs were crashing, while Beasley and Breckenridge were shouting, "Keep Calm. Everybody stay where they are." Off to one side, the band seized the opportunity to break into an impromptu rendition of "*Tiger Rag*."

As the clamor mounted, Vernon Grover stood up in the melee and shouted, "Gung Ho! Damn the torpedoes! Let's get our diplomas!" As one, the entire graduating class rose, pushed on to the stage and assailed the table of rolled certificates, elbowing each other joyously and chanting, "Class of '55! Class of '55!"

Somehow in the mass of confusion Perry found himself once again next to Williams.

"What a way to go, eh, Perry? I'll bet Sherwood's happy he didn't have to give that corny speech Beasely approved."

The home movie was still rolling, but one of the janitors had switched the lights back on. As Perry tried to refocus his eyes, the first thing he saw was a collapsed chair with Superintendent Breckenridge sitting in the lap of one very irate Mrs. Fitzmorris.

Perry knew this had to be the work of The Mouse. Perry recalled their conversation back in November. "Well, Mouse," he said aloud, "I have to admit you were right. We sure will remember you for a lot more than your bad teeth."

June, 1955 News Flashes

Walt Disney's feature-length cartoon, "Lady and the Tramp," opens in New York City.

North Vietnamese President Ho Chi Minh arrives in Peking at the start of a two-week state visit.

"Smog" or "poisoned air" becomes a public concern.

A scientist named Gregory Pincus is said to have discovered a substance that will lead to the development of an oral contraceptive pill for women.

Epilogue

Johnson was clearly agaitated. In the muted light of Williams basement he paced furiously and waved the rolled up newspaper over his head like a conductor's baton. "Did you lamebrains see this story about McIntyre? Can you believe it? Turns out Old Lady Fitzmorris wasn't so whacko after all."

Perry, sitting on the edge of Williams unmade bed, yawned. "Hey, take it easy," he said. "It's June, the sun's shining, the birds are singing, and we all ended up with the right diplomas. McIntyre and all the rest of those teachers are out of our lives."

Sherwood reached out from his perch on the stairway and grabbed the newspaper from Johnson. "Yeah, why bug us about some society page gossip? Who purloined the sports section?"

Johnson lunged back at Sherwood and tore off the page he had been reading. "This makes me puke," he sputtered. "Listen to this garbage: 'August nuptials planned by New Rose lovebirds. Local community leaders, Mr. And Mrs. Finley Kelly, announce the engagement of their daughter, Amber, to Mr. Rodney McIntyre, son of Mr. and Mrs. Ambrose McIntyre of Puyallup, Washington. Vows will be exchanged in a gala wedding ceremony in Blue Lake Park this coming August, with a reception to follow at Gendoveer Golf Club. The groom plans to coach in California, next year, and the bride will attend junior college, majoring in theater arts.' Ah, horse puckey!" He wadded up the paper and hurled it at Perry.

"Hey, big deal. It's a free country," said Kingfisher, who was slouching in a corner and pulling stray hairs from his pocket comb.

"Think we'll get invited to the wedding?" asked Williams who suddenly appeared, bounding down the stairs and leaping over Sherwood. He was wearing his American Legion baseball jersey over his faded jeans.

"Who cares?" was Johnson's response.

"I care," shouted Perry. "It's an opportunity for free food and drink. Why not go?"

"Think Beasely will get an invitation?" snickered Williams.

"Didn't you hear?" inquired Kingfisher as he brushed stray hairs from his sleeve. "Beasely's gone. In fact, real gone! After the school board demanded his resignation, he left town pronto. They say he's taken a job in Samoa. Probably will end up wearing a grass skirt."

"Good riddance," mumbled Sherwood. "His licentious behavior was appalling."

"Did he take Frenchy with him?" asked Perry.

Kingfisher rolled his eyes. "Oh, that's another good one. After she left, my dad found out she wasn't exactly the exchange student we though she was. Turns out she's actually 21 years old, and was working undercover as a reporter for a Paris scandal magazine. She was here to dig up a story on sex and booze in a typical American public high school. Beasely may end up sharing the cover of their August issue with Brigitt Bardot, the French sex kitten."

Johnson pointed a finger at Perry. "Did the old greaseball ever come through with that scholarship he dangled in front of you?"

"No. Actually I'm not sure he really had the influence he claimed with the Woodhall decision makers. Anyhow, the scholarship went to Freida Lewick.

But that's okay. I got a donation from the Mother's Club, and it doesn't cost all that much to go to college here in New Rose. The big drawback is having to live at home, but with a bit of luck I might get an apartment." He paused and shook his head. "And guess who I might be sharing it with? None other than The Mouse! He's already enrolled and plans to major in Creative Film Making.

Perry sat back on his favorite old wooden chair and took a long look at the cluttered half basement and its occupants. Williams had picked up his leather fielders' mitt, and was rubbing greasy oil into it. Sherwood once again was rooting through Williams' stack of old *National Geographics*. Kingfisher had retrieved the remnants of the *Oregonian* and was reading headlines. Johnson, still miffed by the actions of coach McIntryre, was glumly staring at a dangling spider.

Perry started to say something more about college, but stopped because it made him realize that very soon everyone in this musty den would be going a separate way. Before long, the arguments, the conversations, the schemes of this quintet would be reduced to memories. He knew Sherwood had a ROTC scholarship to a college downstate, and Johnson was thinking of joining the Merchant Marine. Kingfisher had applied to a number of universities and was going to pick the one which "offered the best array of coed pulchritude, to use a word approved by Sherwood." And Williams had offers from several junior college baseball coaches.

A momentary wave of sadness swept over Perry, along with a sense of impending loss. He had known it couldn't last forever, this regular gathering of kindred spirits, but still he was surprised that it was coming to a close so soon.

Surely there would never be another year like the one they just experienced.

His mind conjured up memories of golf flags (good grief, I wonder if they are still gathering dust in the chicken house?), football games, Rocky Butte episodes, Mad Friday, poison oak and of course, the ever-alluring-but-aloof Franscoise. It had been a great time to be alive. "I suppose this is what they mean when they talk about brotherhood," he thought. "Without a doubt these guys are the best family I've ever known." He chuckled. "And this hole is the one place where I never feel cold, even if it's icicle city outside."

He wondered what the future would hold for all of them. Would they stay in touch or drift away never to be united again? Would they ever have friends who meant so much and asked so little in return? Would they ever have so many laughs? "Probably not," he mumbled. He tried to get hold of his feelings, to fully grasp the meaning of this moment, but his brief epiphany was short-lived.

Johnson was in his face, so close Perry could smell his breath and see the hairs in his nostrils. "What are you mumbling about, Pearhead? Come on, Let's do something. Anything! The minutes of our lives are ticking away."

Printed in the United States
34620LVS00002B/184-231